Seatack, Virginia

The Untold Stories

M. E.

ARCHWAY PUBLISHING

Archway Publishing books may be ordered through booksellers or by contacting:

Archway Publishing
1663 Liberty Drive
Bloomington, IN 47403
www.archwaypublishing.com
1 (888) 242-5904

Interior Image Credit: Morris Albritton

ISBN: 978-1-4808-9160-9 (sc)
ISBN: 978-1-4808-9161-6 (e)

Library of Congress Control Number: 2020910422

Print information available on the last page.

Archway Publishing rev. date: 6/26/2020

ACKNOWLEDGEMENTS

FIRST OF ALL, I WOULD like to give thanks to God and his son Jesus from which all blessings flow. Secondly, love is not powerful enough to scratch the surface of my mother's worth, in my life, to her family... the world. We can never repay our parents. If I lived a hundred life times over, I could never soothe even a small portion of the heartaches I've caused "Murr Lee" as she is often referred to..... still she loves me unconditionally. Thank you, Mary Lee Vaughan-Edmonds.

..........this one here is for, and inspired by you..

CONTENTS

FOREWORD

THE DEPICTION SEEN ON THE front cover once hung inside the Chrysler museum in Norfolk,Virginia under an exhibit called "Beyond the block",from November 2019 to February of 2020. The illustrator was kind enough to lend it to me for my humble endeavor.It shows pain,suffering,will,and triumph. Amendment 13,14, and 15 is the title and each of these constitutional amendments directly refers to the abolishment of slavery. The artist, while incarcerated,was only permitted to have a flimsy ink pen no longer than the length of the average middle digit of the human hand. Out of this disadvantage a piece worthy of public display was created,just as,out of slavery came the ideology of freedom,and so the rebuttal mass incarceration was birthed. I firmly believe when given lemons in life you make lemonade. When given a piece of pen,handcuffs,and shackles what can be made?

Well,the front cover,the contents in between it,and the back are proof of the proverbial silver lining. I wrote this entire book while incarcerated. I am an unorthodox oxymoron who's often ambidextrous in thought,and action. I was told "not to do that",or "I should do this", yet, I've always done it my way like Mr. Frank Sinatra.

There is structure included, simply put there are rules that govern all things,the literary world is of no exception. I chopped,minced,impaled, sliced, diced, and crammed my passion,belief, soul, thought,and core being between each line. So if you notice a few lines warped,bowed,or not plumb you know why.

As a young impressionable mind Seatack was an enchanted,magical place filled with love,unity,and proudness. I can only compare it to any of the great fairy tales you may have read that begin with the words "Once Upon a time" take your pick, when everything in that story was deemed perfect. Of course a lot of change had taken place in the 80 years or more between it's beginning in the 1900 and the 1980's I had the pleasure of experiencing.

As a child growing up everyone knew your last name,your family,and looked out for one another by treating each other as family. Today it is more common to look out for yourself,avoid, condemn, and conspire against others. It was natural to help people, speak to, and welcome strangers. The use of "yes sir", and "no ma'am" several times a day, being on your best behavior, and manners weren't mandatory but simply normalcy.

Struggle was expected,not a gripe but an accepted way of life that became easier with each day we gained footing in any area of advancement as a fortified unit, and we then had 80 years or more of historical success to prove it.

Seatack was made up of proud spiritual people who made the best of what they had, and loved to see others progress no matter race, creed, color, or sex.

The spirit of Seatack was loud, unique, vibrant, intoxicating, loving, caring, and most of all contagious!

Families were intertwined through blood or marriage, sometimes by near proximity of forged relationships. Today I am trying to instill the same core values though at least a century outdated, in my children. Just like those values the area has changed drastically in the last 100 years. Surprisingly enough there are still residents around who remember, exude, and practice the soul of Seatack.

This is my humble attempt to pay homage, thank Seatack for all it gave, and sacrificed while helping to raise me.

It has been said "it takes a village to raise a child". I was raised by 12 (2 grandparents, my mother, four aunts, and five uncles).

Seatack was the village of villagers who believed, taught, and practiced identical principles, integrity, morals, etc....

I am so saddened by the fact many of you readers,especially my children, will never experience this great Golden era I speak of. However, we can rebuild and recreate. This is my contribution, how will you choose to help build a better world?

INTRO

In case you didn't know

IN THE EARLY 1900S, THE name Seatack specifically applied to an area west of Virginia Beach, the oldest neighborhood of free black slaves in Princess Anne County. Legend has it blacks were allowed to settle in this area because whites saw no future value in the swampy wooded land. Blacks not only settled this area but also thrived there. Blacks(such as my grandparents)who lived in the area called Seatack made many historical accomplishments in the segregated county of Princess Anne, that included raising money to build schools for their children (namely, Princess Anne County Training School—1938), starting a fire station (Seatack Fire Station) because the black neighborhood wasn't serviced by the city fire and rescue, building churches (Mount Olive Baptist, Saint Stephen's COGIC) to worship in, and a community/ daycare center.

PROLOGUE

1977-1978

"I CAN'T BELIEVE THIS..... HOW could she?"

"Bartender, can I get another round over here?" His vision was distorted, hearing impaired, and each word slurred more than the one before.

"Okay, pal, you had enough. I could see you had some problems coming in the door so I made an exception to the rules. We don't serve your kind in here, look around, you're disturbing the patrons. So why don't you wait outside while I call you a cab, Bubba?"

Unable to move right away, he sat still to steady himself on the barstool while staring at the Confederate flag hanging on the wall behind the bar that seemed to be taunting him.

"Get out of here, nigger!"

"Yeah, befo we hang yo black ass!" Someone yelled to reinforce the previous warning. A bottle was thrown, hitting him in the back of the head. Blood and small shards of glass were all he could see in his hand after feeling the back of his head. Survival instincts took over. A quick, short chop to the throat of the closest racist rendered the man helpless on the floor, holding his neck with both hands firmly while gasping for air. Immediately, with a sharp pivot, the first punch was thrown in the opposite direction, breaking another attacker's jaw on impact. He proceeded to grab the bartender by the collar and head-butt him on the bridge of the nose before being overpowered.... forced to succumb to the extreme darkness that came rushing in.

CHAPTER ONE

1978

THE 1977 HUNTER GREEN FORD Thunderbird came with flip-up headlights, white pinstripes running down both sides of the frame, white wall tires, hunter green vinyl ragtop, velour suede seats, 8-track cassette player, and oval rear windows with Thunderbird emblems etched into the glass. Michael Perry, known to everyone as Mike Mike had peddled enough small manila envelopes of heroin to finally purchase his dream ride. Although he was a year late, it was a start, a status symbol if you will. The Mean Streets of Washington DC had been tough over the years but more recently had become generous. Michael had gone from lookout, to runner, and now a partner in the drug trade hierarchy. His mother Elaine moved to Virginia but he refused to leave the city for the slow wiles of the country, such as thick women, fresh produce and clean air. He had a reputation for having a quick temper, fast hard hitting hands, and carrying a buck knife with Old Hickory carved in the dark brown handle. The buck knife had a hook blade that allowed its victims to be pulled in close, stabbed, and then ripped apart by the hook of the blade on its way out, spilling all innards not caught by the victim's hand, or held inside by muscle tissue. The murder of his partner and multiple attempts on his life left one option... Elaine.

Elaine Perry prided herself on being a strong, self-sufficient black woman. At thirty-one she stood five feet, and weighed one hundred and twenty pounds. This was all lean muscle. Her physique was lingerie model worthy but remained hidden under a variety of uniforms provided by several employees over the years. Elaine's long black hair was almost always in a ponytail held by a scrunchie. Her long narrow face and piercing eyes added to the homely yet serious impression she projected.

At the tender age of 14 she allowed herself to be sucked in by the charms of a street hustler named Michael. Once it became apparent he ran women, had no intention of marrying her, being a family man, having a relationship with his son, or leaving the streets alone, she decided to do it all by herself. She accepted welfare during her pregnancy and only when times got extremely rough. Working two or three jobs was normal for her. Elaine vowed to never let another man have the sort of power over her Michael Senior had once been given.

Her worst fear was having Michael Junior turn out to be just like his father. When she received the call informing her of all the trouble he was mixed up in, she knew the city would do to him what it had done to his father many years prior, freeze his heart and steal his soul.

"Michael Lavelle Perry Junior... oh there you are. No wonder you can't hear me, you got that damn TV up so loud. Surprised you can hear at all. I guess that's why you didn't pick me up from work, huh? Either you didn't hear my call over the volume, or you were too caught up in watching The Jeffersons! I thought I told you about smoking them cigarettes in my house?" Elaine scolded while swatting the air filled with smoke from in front of her face.

"Cigars ma, King Edward cigars cost a grip in da city," he informed her. She was frustrated from standing on her feet twelve hours cleaning hotel rooms, then catching multiple bus transfers, only to find her son watching TV instead of easing the day by picking her up. Elaine picked the dark brown lit cigarette up by her index finger and thumb before dropping it in the toilet and flushing. "Now, I agree to let you come down here to get a new start, not lay around and make things harder for me."

"I'm sorry I didn't get your call, Mom. I have been looking for a job which is probably when you called. You ain't have to flush my cigar Joe?"

"Yeah, you're too young to be smoking that shit, besides I got you a job with me so we won't have any more transportation or phone call problems… and what I tell you about that Joe shit?"

*

The Sundial Motel could be found at the corner of 21st Street and Pacific Avenue, right behind McDonalds. It sat on large cement columns which allowed parking directly underneath the actual structure. 21st Street was an extension of the interstate's one-way traffic to the oceanfront. The front office housed cleaning parts and supplies on the right side of the parking lot while the guest rooms were found on the left. Michael's job was to aide the maintenance man, once one was hired for the position. In the meantime he would be required to help any maid in need of assistance. The oceanfront area was filled with seasonal hiring signs, tourists, including kids on summer break, and great weather.

*

"Welcome to McDonald's, may I take your order?"

Michael was instantly lost in the soft voice that spoke from between such a perfect set of white teeth.

"Excuse me sir, you're holding up the line. If you need time to decide which value meal you want,please step to the side and I will come back to you."

He stepped to the side without uttering a word. Michael watched as customer after customer placed orders during the lunch rush hour. Finally, he realized if he didn't go through another line he'd miss the whole lunch hour and his stomach would remind him the rest of the day.

Smitten

Michael finally placed an order and found a secluded spot away from the other customers dining in.

"Hi, mind if I join you, or were you expecting someone?"

Michael shook his head to signal he wasn't waiting for anyone because his mouth was filled with the remnants of a Big Mac. He knew he was running late the first day on the job and here was this gorgeous female muddling every thought in his head.

"Did that mean no, you don't mind, or no, you're not expecting anyone? You don't seem to be big on conversation, are you?"

"Seems you do enough talking for us both," Michael said before he knew it.

She placed her fish fillet sandwich down neatly on the tray and stared curiously into Michael's eyes. "Fair enough. You aren't from around here. What's your name and where you from?"

"My name is Mike and I'm from Washington D.C., Northwest."

"Okay. Well, I'm Vanessa, pleased to meet you Mike from DC," she said in a sarcastic tone before smiling.

"Vanessa, I should have known," Mike responded before scooting back in the booth they were sharing.

"You should have known, what you mean by that?" she asked with obvious hurt in her tone.

"Feisty, huh? It was a compliment. A pretty name for a pretty female, that's all. Don't beat me up. So how old are you?"

"Just turned 16 a few days ago. I hate to cut this short but my lunch break is almost over and my manager don't play checking in late. Nice meeting you, Mike from DC." Vanessa said before quickly dumping her tray and disappearing through an employee-only door behind the cashier's counter.

Mike just sat still and watched her long black silky hair that curled at the ends bounce around as she read receipts and filled orders. The black plastic hair band pulling back her hair allowed it to swing just inches from her face before being restrained. Her soft caramel skin reflected light perfectly while her enticing hazel eyes caused Mike to lose himself in them. Her soft thin lips accented her smile and made him envision pressing his lips against them. Every so often they made eye contact and she would smile in a quick shy manner while shuffling through some work task.

"Shit, I'm late!" Mike blurted out after noticing the clock behind the register Vanessa was working. He almost knocked a few customers down rushing out the front door and transitioning into a full sprint.

*

"Get out of that damn mirror. Shit. I don't see what all the fuss is about. Got the whole house smelling like we bottle and package British Sterling cologne. How much of that shit did you put on anyway? Come here let me see you. Let me look at you. You look so nice. Don't let that girl make you late for work tomorrow morning," Elaine rambled on while fixing Michael's collar with proud tears of happiness in both eyes.

Mike wore a dark brown butterfly collar shirt, Blue Bell Bottom Braxton jeans, dark brown turkey toe shoes and a brown Fedora with a tan band wrap with matching tan leather belt. Every surface that cast a reflection made him pause to check his appearance.

He had long learned Elaine was in denial concerning his dealings in the street and the fact he was no longer a little boy. He chalked it up as guilt over her not being able to be there because of constant work hours when he was younger. The fuss she made over the smallest things and smothering his private space and affairs, such as unsolicited advice for this date, was overlooked for these reasons.

"Michael, when can I meet her? Make sure you take her someplace nice, open doors, pull out her chair like I taught you... show home training. Let her know southern hospitality don't just come from the country. City slickers know a thing or two."

"Okay, Mom, see you later," Michael responded with a comical grin while shaking his head as he walked out of the door.

*

"Hey, go, go, go before my mom comes out of the bathroom! She's all anxious to meet you for some reason. I know she's going to embarrass me by pulling out old baby pictures or telling you something I did when I was little that should never be discussed ever again. She'll ask about family and other stuff that you wouldn't even ask in-laws," Vanessa explained.

"So, you got a problem with me meeting your mom, or is this just your way of saying something else?... Nah, I'm just kidding. My mom has been giving me hell ever since we met. She's been coming to your job for lunch trying to figure out which cashier you are. That's why I come in different times now," Michael explained to Vanessa with a smile of relief.

"Well that phone booth across from my house is where we'll meet from now on until we are ready for all that. By the way, why you keep calling me Joe?"

"Oh, that's a DC thing, like man or girl or you get what I mean, Joe?"

"I guess… Joe," Vanessa said in a comical manner, and took notice of Michael's slight irritation.

Woo

Seatack Park sat right off Birdneck Road. A dark maroon painted sign made of planked fencing wood with white painted letters introduce its existence to visitors and passerbys. The parking lot was filled with rocks and fenced off by large, dark brown, rotted beach logs that gave it character. Small poles with chains running in between them served as a separation from the park and parking lot. To the left of the park was a small children's section consisting of merry-go-round, a small swing with bucket seating and opening for legs, see-saw, and small animal characters attached to a large spring used for rocking purposes. Each of these areas was dug out and sand placed all around the base. Straight ahead was a basketball court. To the right of it, picnic tables and grills with a roof built above it for weather protection. To the left, a baseball field. The rest of the small community park was grass surrounded by woods.

"Clink, this is so nice and secluded. How did you know about this place?" Vanessa asked after touching her 16 oz glass bottle of coke against his, while sharing a large slice of Domino's extra cheese pizza with black olives.

"How about you tell me why Domino's and why extra cheese and black olives had to be added no matter what?" Mike asked with amusement. The pink, peach, lavender, violent, gray, purple and blue hues of the sunset faded into each other to form a perfect natural Northern lights landscape.

"This is truly amazing. Now, how many girls have you brought out here?" Vanessa asked before biting her lip in anticipation of his reply.

"I just found this place a few days ago so I haven't had the chance to break it in yet, but give me a couple of days, Joe."

Vanessa reached over and punched him in his left arm with her fist while they lay on their backs. Soon they held hands and enjoyed the view as the sounds of the woods added to the romantic scene.

"What are you thinking?"

"I don't know. Why are girls always thinking so much? I'm just enjoying this time with you, Joe."

"I don't know. I really like you and I wanted to know if you wanted to maybe go steady? That's all" Vanessa asked nervously.

Mike sat up and Vanessa followed. He gently placed his leather coat around her shoulders then cradled her face and slid his tongue into her mouth. After thoroughly massaging each others tongues, Mike simply answered, "Of course I do, Joe." Then he placed his hat on her head and touched the tip of her nose affectionately with his index finger.

Formality

2014

"Good morning. You are Michael Perry, correct? Inmate #1163782, currently serving a forty-five-year sentence for murder, of which you have served twenty-seven consecutive years. Is this accurate so far, Mr. Perry?"

"Yeah, but I don't want parole. I was sleep and they made me come anyway."

"Duly noted, Mr. Perry, and if you will just bear with me a little while longer. I will make sure you are able to get back to whatever it is you were doing. I see here, there was a pattern of institutional infractions that seem to have changed dramatically over the last few years. Care to comment?"

"No. Let's speed this shit up, will ya?"

"We're almost done. Language, Mr. Perry. I'm moving as fast as I can, sir. I see where you've completed several programs, trades, and even helped inmates obtain their G.E.D. as a teacher's aide. Good for you. All the correct answers lie here before me in these here folders, as it has been the past... going on 6 years, according to the dates logged. I usually ask why you think the parole board should grant parole. Instead, I would like to know if you have accepted responsibility for the crimes you have committed, Mr. Perry? Let the record reflect the inmate is unresponsive. I think I have enough for the board to review and make a decision. This concludes the interview with inmate Michael Perry, state number 1163782. I am now about to turn the tape recorder off. Is there anything you would like to add that the parole board may need to know before making a final decision?"

"No."

"Well... thank you for your patience. We will contact you with a decision through your counselor. Have a nice day. Officer, please escort Mr. Perry back to his building and send the next person in, please."

Michael Perry, AKA "Mike Mike" lost everything of importance to him during the more recent seven years of his incarceration. His dignity, time, youth, and freedom were a small price to pay. Losing the love of his life, and then his mother, caused him to shut down all emotional and social interactions. He remained adamant about being innocent, railroaded by his public defender, and the justice system as a whole through the use of the Appeals Court, which denied his self-defense grounds. Parole turn downs were a small matter, to be expected every year.

CHAPTER TWO

1987

THE SUMMER HELD FEW WORRIES in the mind of sixteen year old Bradford Williams. Life consisted of helping his grandfather pick tomatoes from the garden, and being rewarded with a little salt to sprinkle on the biggest ones to cool off the heat, in his mind that is. Snap beans also grew in the garden but required more time and effort. He didn't mind it at all on occasions, except the process meant sitting indoors on a nice summer day that was designed strictly for playing, not using precious hours preparing dinner with his mother.

Two stainless steel bowls out of the three-piece set that ranged in different sizes, allowing them to fit perfectly inside each other, where used. The large bowl was filled with water where his mother would snap stemmed branches. Bradford would mimic these actions over the other bowl filled with water to rinse away any dirt, pesticides or insects. He also enjoyed playing on the all grey primer tractor that drove with a sort of gallop like a horse, or simply climbing crabapple trees for fruit. This turned into throwing the fruit or gorging away until a tummy ache ensued.

The use of water guns, cap guns, and BB guns were a neighborhood pastime every young boy participated in except Bradford. His mother believed this was a gateway to encouraging the use of real guns. Wrestling, Kung Fu cartoons, and football were the next best thing. Most of the time there weren't enough kids out at the same time to start a full game so they played "Smear the Queer." This game involved one person running the football against the whole field of players. Every day a new way to start a fight was found and games were no exception. Whoever caught the ball would be run into a tree, thrown into the street, or tacked onto the cement. This was a touchy situation because sometimes the ball would be thrown by someone specific so a few others who already conspired together could jump on him and beat him up. This kind of thing was a common occurrence but if you weren't from the neighborhood everyone would jump you. Joking, debates, and sports turned into black eyes, bloody noses, and a tighter friendship the following day. Bradford's mother Monica often separated him from these situations after a fight, unable to see it was a necessity to gain acceptance. A rite of passage.

Adolescence

"Boy, who you been fighting now?" Sabrina asked as she opened the front door, letting Bradford in and heading back towards the kitchen. She wore all black biking tights and a white T-shirt tied around her waist in a knot exposing her firm flat stomach. Sabrina had radiant chestnut skin accentuated by a plump ass that Bradford couldn't resist feeling even though she slapped him enough times, trying to convince him to stop. Sabrina was Bradford's upstairs neighbor who was more the tomboy/sister type. They were very close, so he often hid things to prevent worry or a lecture, not this particular time though.

"Tasha did it!" Bradford blurted out, referring to the black eye and scratches on his face. He knew Sabrina would beat Tasha up so he took full advantage of this fact. His mother didn't allow him to hit girls no matter the circumstances.

"I got you, Brad. Her black burnt skinny ass always starting trouble and can't fight a lick," Sabrina huffed while standing over the stove cooking "steak ums." She'd gotten into a few strained conversations with Tasha on the bus before. The kind that told Tasha, Sabrina was not the one she wanted to tangle with at all!

Bradford could tell she was deep in thought. He couldn't help but notice she wasn't wearing any panties under the material that hugged her firm, soft, shapely body. He couldn't resist a second longer. He saw the opportunity and seized it by quickly caressing her left butt cheek with his left hand and moving from an arms-length distance to avoid her reflex swing.

"You don't learn, do you?" Sabrina said with a smirk as she went into the refrigerator and pulled out a long square cardboard box filled with thick reddish orange colored welfare cheese. Bradford never understood why Sabrina's mom had the same embarrassing products of poverty and shame found in his house. He would jump at the opportunity to watch cable upstairs with Sabrina whenever his mother had an errand or two to run. The hallway door downstairs could always be heard opening and shutting no matter the noise level upstairs in Sabrina's apartment. Bradford would quickly check the blinds in the living room of Sabrina's apartment to see if his mother's car was parked in front of the building, in case he heard the door slam. If he took too long, she yelled his name in the hallway. "Bradford!!!"

"See you later, Sabrina," Bradford said while darting towards the door.

"That's for feeling my butt," she said with a playful rib shot that knocked a little wind from his lungs.

*

Bradford earned the name "Church boy" because he attended church more than the collection plates used in the actual church offerings. This was not a good thing all of a sudden. He couldn't understand why there was a vast difference in the adult world standards, and the world he existed in. The neighborhood girls varied in size, shape, color, and temperament. The one thing they all had in common was not letting him hump them. Sabrina was his testing ground for nastiness, although his arm or other body parts paid the price for his lasciviousness. Every girl wanted a commitment or to "go together" on their terms. This required holding hands, passing love notes, and messages through other people, kissing, etc... All of this was done so eventually she would pull down her panties and allow experimentation from an inexperienced hormonal boyfriend. He would later find the adult world was not so different after all.

Cora, who lived across the street, didn't need all of those requirements. She was known as "easy" and had taken a newfound interest in Bradford which was crazy because she had previously taken pleasure in beating him up. Bradford was always rated cute by the neighbourhood girls, and those attending school with him, via Sabrina's inquiring. The problem was peer-pressure. Since he was called "Church boy" and couldn't afford the latest "must have" trends, he wasn't an acceptable choice in most circles. Somehow Cora saw past all this. Whatever it was she saw in him was unimportant to him, as long as she pulled her pants down for him as she had reportedly done for more than half the neighborhood.

"What's up Cora?" Bradford said through the screen of the half-raised window in his living room. Cora had piercing light brown eyes that were slightly slanted. She had perfect white teeth with a Jheri curl that required greasing around the hairline. Cora had on all white K-Swiss sneakers, stonewashed jeans, and a K-Swiss t-shirt.

"Nothing. I ain't seen your mama's car so I came to see if I can play your Atari," she said quite frankly while rolling her eyes and smiling.

"Where yo room at?" Cora asked after walking through his house as soon as he let her in.

"I thought we were playing the game? You gotta come back up front in case my momma come home early," Bradford said, while following her nervously.

"Okay, we can go to my house cause my momma ain't home. She at her boyfriend's house doing the nasty," Cora calmly said after satisfying her curiosity to see his room.

"I can't leave, my mom will kill me if I get caught," said Bradford pitifully.

"DAGGG.... yo momma mean. Alright then," Cora said before kissing Bradford on the lips unprompted. She unzipped her jeans and pulled them off, then she took off her shirt, bra, and panties. Bradford was still stunned by the kiss.

"Boy, come on befo yo momma come back," she said after smacking her lips in irritation.

Bradford timidly fondled, caressed and stroked her developing breasts. He stared between her legs, which to him looked like two fingers curled under to form a fist. It was soft and wet down there. Bradford noticed how Cora opened her legs and used her hands to guide his. A primal urge took over, causing him to get down on his knees and kiss it. She turned around and he kissed her ass too. The smell on his fingers was foreign except for a slight stench of urine.

"Pull it out and stick it in," Cora instructed while bending over on the couch and spreading both cheeks. Bradford pulled down his pants nervously and slid himself between her thighs, just barely wedging between the bottom of her ass cheeks. The heat between her legs excited him instantly. After a few pumps she got up and placed him between her legs while they both stood up facing each other, kissing. Cora pushed her tongue into his mouth aggressively which Bradford thought was gross until he tasted the watermelon jolly rancher she was sucking on. Bradford turned her back around and bent her over. He pulled his finger between her vaginal lips in a come here motion while sniffing her ass and kissing it all over.

"What's this," Bradford asked after finding her pink opening and sticking his finger inside.

"Ouch!" she said while jumping and removing his finger. "That hurt!" Cora explained with tears in her eyes as she quickly got dressed.

"I'm sorry... I didn't know," Bradford replied.

"Don't worry about it, we'll do it again later, but first let's play this game," Cora said with renewed excitement.

Bradford quickly loaded the asteroids cartridge into the Atari 2600 game console and switched from the area of uncertainty to his area of expertise. Cora's snickers could barely be heard over the video game but not only did Bradford hear them, it added further insult to the injury of losing to a girl. "Take that and this... and that... don't get quiet now," Cora taunted as her score continued to rise.

"How did you know how to play?"

"I've got this game at home, duh," she answered, enjoying the pain clearly written across his face after the pain he had caused her with his finger.

"So, why you come over here to play my game?" Bradford asked because of his injured pride more than anything.

"To do the Oochie Coochie with you.... silly," she revealed while continuing to beat him without mercy.

"Oh snap, my mom just pulled up. Go hide in my room, then I'll sneak you out."

"Yeah right. You'll say anything to distract me so you can win, cheater," Cora fired back unable to hear the fear in Bradford's voice over her own determination to gloat. Hearing the keys unlocking the bottom and top locks from the outside of the front door sent Cora into a quick sprint towards his bedroom.

"Hey, I left some things in the car for you to bring in," Monica informed him while rushing by headed straight to the bathroom. "Boy, how many times I gotta tell you to leave the toilet seat down!" she screamed after falling in.

"I'm sorry, ma," Bradford said in a remorseful tone before sneaking into his room. "Come on," he whispered to Cora as he took her hand and led her from his room into the living room then out the front door. They both stopped once safely outside in front of Monica's 1969 Cobalt Blue Chevy Nova that all of the kids called "The Cookie Monster" and busted out laughing with their little hearts still racing. Bradford was confused, not knowing whether it was because his mother had fallen in the toilet, the fact she almost caught them and they got away, or their first little botched sexual experience together.

"Next time we can do it at my house. My mom has Playboy and nasty beta tapes we can watch and try stuff," Cora said before waving goodbye as she walked slowly back across the court.

"Next time," was all Bradford heard her say, and it kept replaying in his mind as he grabbed the bags left in his mother's car.

CHAPTER THREE

VIRGINIA BEACH JUNIOR HIGH WAS located between 24th and 25th Street. The school motto the Seahawks, trimmed in emerald green and white, was a part of a proud tradition passed down to anyone coming behind the Seniors. This was mostly pertaining to sports, which Bradford had a few skills in but knew his mother Monica would never approve of. He could hear her now. "I'm having a hard enough time making ends meet, raising you all by myself. Feet keep growing... not gone be sitting in nobody mergency room and you all broke up." As a freshman starting seventh grade in a new school, Bradford felt like an exchange student rather than resident. He often roamed the halls observing and avoiding signs of trouble, seeking new interests, daydreaming, or simply being late for class. The lunchroom was a different story. There were tables you were invited to only, tables that troublemakers sat at, the "in-crowd" tables, and the "nobody cares to know you" misfits table.

"Ah, y'all check this out. He got Adidas on with four stripes. Look like bobos to me... what yall think?!!!"

Bradford heard the comment and instantly felt sorry for whoever was being picked on. He hated bullies, besides, he also had on bobos, which was basically what any shoe worn that didn't cost more than twenty dollars was called. Suddenly he remembered he had on the four striped shoes being mentioned and looked up from his tray with a mouth full of french fries to a room packed with eyes staring back at him. Bradford wanted to climb under the table. He picked his tray up, still filled with food and threw it away. He never caught a glimpse of the voice responsible for the taunting. Someone stuck their leg out and tripped him, creating instant laughter throughout the lunchroom, until he sprang up and punched the owner square in the nose. Blood sprayed everywhere on impact.

"Fight, fight, fight!" The crowd chanted as they surrounded the two fighters.

Bradford had no idea he had just hit the Regional wrestling State Champion and Captain of the school's Wrestling team. The taller muscular boy went into a training drill on reflex and raw adrenaline. Unable to see, he grabbed Bradford in a blind panic and slammed him across a lunch table. Before Bradford could recover, security rushed in the cafeteria.

"Stop right there you, you should know better. That's enough, both of you," the uniformed men instructed and scolded as they removed both boys from the cafeteria.

*

The wait to see the assistant principal, due to the principle being too busy to tend to such trivial things, was filled with unease and uncertainty. The large front office area had several different doors that ran along a corridor, one being the assistant principal's office, which was extremely busy. Students ran in and out, either making announcements on the P.A. system, or held absent excuse notes from home concerning the previous day or week. Between bells, students who saw the fight or were friends of the bully peeked in and punched the palms of their hands to signal there would be more trouble outside the office.

"Don't worry about my boys; it's squashed between us... besides, my coach is gone have my ass, and they don't want none of what I'm gonna get."

Bradford looked over at his opponent with disdain while the guy held a sky blue rubber bag filled with ice against his nose. Since his head was tilted back, compliments of the nurse, Bradford wrestled with the thought of hitting him again but thought better of it.

"My name is Larry, freshman. It wasn't personal but you had it coming. You had to know better than to wear dem shoes... not on the first day," Larry said then extended his hand to shake while laughing.

Bradford saw nothing funny at all but shook his hand to build a façade of camaraderie while trying to figure out how to put a spin on the whole story.

Mr. Grindle walked in casually, looking like a middle aged Henry Winkler. He had a no-nonsense presence and expression, which meant he'd dealt with Larry before, and the best course of action was going to be playing with an innocent look, the lack of facts, and the "new kid first-time" pass.

"It was a misunderstanding. Someone threw something in the lunchroom and it hit me in the nose. I tried to get out of the way of whatever was going on because I couldn't see. I ran into him and knocked him across the lunch table in the process," Larry began without being asked.

"Is that correct Mr... Uh, Wiliams?" Mr. Grindle asked with obvious disbelief in his voice.

"Uh...Yeah... I guess. I'm still trying to figure out what happened. I don't know him or why we're even here," Bradford said with an innocent face.

"I see... I'm going to go against everything telling me to suspend the both of you on the first day of school. I seriously doubt that load of horse shit that just came out of your mouth, Larry, but I don't feel like dealing with parents and paperwork today. So, you two get back to wherever you should be during sixth period."

*

Bradford and Larry formed an unspoken bond of respect for each other after the makeshift story ended up working. The unwritten traditional rules stated seniors hazed freshmen and never ate or hung with them. Larry was never good at following rules, especially those that encouraged making fun of those less fortunate. They would briefly speak in passing or give a quick head nod in the confines of school walls. Now that fate had played a cruel trick of introducing them, Bradford noticed Larry was everywhere. Sabrina was also a senior who broke the invisible rules by hanging with Bradford. Larry had a crush on her and would ask Bradford to hook them up after he made the mistake of saying there was nothing other than a friendship between him and her. Bradford was against the thought before he was asked. He told himself it was all the girls Larry had, but there was more to it... much more.

"I got a note from Larry today saying he wants to go to the school dance. He said he sent a few messages through somebody but won't tell me who. You wouldn't know anything about this would you?" Sabrina asked Bradford with a look that conveyed amusement, accusation, anger, and curiosity all at the same time.

"I gotta go. Another tardy in this class means detention. Monica ain't going for that."

Unexpected

Sabrina and Larry became an item. Bradford was unsure if his elusiveness contributed or not, and it sat with him as well as spoiled milk on an upset stomach. The school dance was a topic that echoed in every hallway, bathroom, and classroom. Bradford had planned to ask Sabrina since Cora no longer lived in the neighborhood but his mother believed the event was "of the devil" as she'd put it, so his hesitation became Larry's window of opportunity. Then he saw her. It was only a quick glance but Bradford was left in a trance. He'd heard a little gossip in the halls and boys locker room about a new girl. Their description didn't even come close to the few seconds his eyes rested on her.

Bradford made his way through the crowds of students headed in different directions after her, except she was long gone. There were too many students scattering for last minute stops at their lockers, a few words with friends, and ultimately to find the right school bus to go home. Bradford heard a faint voice behind him, "hey," turned around, and there she was.

"Excuse me. I'm new here. Can you tell me where to find the buses, or how to find my bus, it's number 829?"

Bradford was unable to force sound from between his lips, and movement was out of the question. Standing before him was the girl he was chasing. Now up close he could see her beautiful almond shaped eyes that were also chinky as if she were of Asian descent.

She had smooth caramel skin, long black hair and a cute button nose that instantly meant love at first sight.

"Well, can you help me or not? I don't wanna miss the bus on the first day, my grandma will kill me."

"I'm sorry. Yeah, I can help you, follow me. By the way, I'm Brad," he said while extending his hand.

"My name's Nicole," she said before shaking his hand and then trying to keep up with his pace, weaving in and out of the stampede of students as the last bell rang.

They both made it on the bus in time. Coincidently they rode the same bus but had to sit in separate seats because they were last and it was crowded. Bradford sat in the back, bypassing a front seat so she could have it. He made sure to lift up from his seat at every stop, over the taller kids seated in front of him, to see where she got off. He wished they were sitting together so he could find out more about her, other than a name and her grandma lived with her. He began imagining her being his date for the school dance even though he wasn't allowed to go... unless... he thought to himself.

The Dance

"I came in the door, said it before, I'll never let the mic......!" Eric B. and Rakim could be heard blaring as soon as you entered the double gym doors of the notorious school dance. Bradford had heard all the stories about them back at Seatack, his elementary school from the juniors, and seniors that would return to see their favorite teachers. Some of them lived in his neighborhood Atlantis and would spread a bit of gossip here and there. The actual event was surreal. Bradford was hypnotized by the different colored lights and circles that could be seen spinning around the floor, walls, and ceiling from the reflection of a large mirrored disco ball centered in the middle of the gym.

Bradford slowly made his way towards the concession tables while his eyes adjusted to the darkness. As soon as he recognized figures dancing it was easy to spot Sabrina and Larry hugged up in a corner. A tap on the shoulder startled him because he'd snuck out the house only intending to stay a minute, maybe get a slow dance and if lucky enough, a kiss.

"Hey, Brad. I can't believe your mom let you out the house. Let's dance, boy!" Cora yelled over the loud music before pulling him onto the dance floor.

"Feeling on booty, check!!," was all his young mind comprehended as she led him into the infamous crowd of young horny teens grinding. Time no longer had a need here.

The night was going better than expected. Bradford usually heard about how much fun school dances were in the lunchroom, bathroom, or on the school bus the following Monday morning. This was much better than all their stories combined with what he'd been told before even starting school. Bradford noticed Sabrina moving in his direction.

Instead of answering questions about how he convinced Monica to let him come, and coming up with a believable lie, or confronting his feelings about their situation, he chose to duck and blend in with the crowd.

"When I'm alone in my room, sometimes I stare at the wall," Bradford heard L.L. Cool J's "I need love" playing and knew it was Sabrina's song, so her and Larry would be headed back to the dance floor to slow grind. This was Larry's chance to feel on her and get away with it, unlike all of his failed attempts. This realization took all the excitement out of his night.

"Hey. I was hoping to see you here because we barely got to talk in school today. We'll have to talk later though cause this my jam," Nicole shouted before dragging Bradford onto the middle of the dance floor.

They slow grinded the entire song. Both of their hormones crashing against each other's body with the intensity of waves thrusting into jagged rocks along the seashore. This overflow of emotion turned into a first kiss for the both of them. The music seemed to keep playing while everyone stood still. This night was so perfect nothing could ruin it.

"So there you are, sneaking out of my house, being fresh and kissing fast tail girls, huh?" Monica fumed before grabbing Bradford by the arm and forcefully removing him from the dance floor and the warm embrace of Nicole's arms. After a series of quick whacks to his head and back he surrendered to the reality that lay before him with the thought, "it was all worth it."

"Just wait till I get you home, negro. Take off everything too... I'm beating naked ass tonight, ain't no clothes!"

CHAPTER FOUR

1989

BRADFORD WOKE UP TO THE familiar sound of the diesel engine downshifting as it took the curve that wrapped around the apartment. Sleep had been virtually impossible all night. Now ten minutes before he should have been walking out the front door, he was greeted with a pleasantly deep sleep. He hopped up, threw on his yellow and black Columbia boots, yellow and black Columbia bubble coat, then checked the full length mirror to make sure the faded light blue "Used" jean outfit wasn't being overshadowed.

A warm pair of strawberry flavored sprinkled Pop Tarts were peeking from the toaster as he gargled Scope mouthwash and spit into the sink before grabbing them and rushing out the front door.

It was clear that the bus stop was packed from at least a block away. The first day of school required the latest styles of hair, clothes, shoes, music, and plenty of conversation. Bradford noticed the different faces, styles and friendships that had been formed and grown over the summer. They were all disappearing through the double doors of the school bus. He ran a little faster and gave up the cute, trying to look cool for the girls jog.

"Hey Brad, you should know I would save a seat for you. I barely saw you all summer. I know working for the summer program made summer less fun than it used to be but it paid off, didn't it? Looking like a Bumble Bee," Sabrina said while pointing to his outfit.

"Yeah," Bradford responded, then pulled one of the pop tarts wrapped in a napkin from his all black Jansport book bag, and offered her the other. This was his way of avoiding the conversation that would eventually lead to, or involve Larry.

The whole summer he would somehow see the two of them and avoid being seen, or be forced to briefly speak while claiming to be running late for some made up prior engagement.

"Larry brought me these, they cute ain't they?" Sabrina asked while smiling from ear to ear, and exposing the large gold plated name earrings.

*

"Go Patriots go! Or, let's go Patriots, Let's go!" was all that could be heard during the first football game of the season in the section Bradford sat in. His high school "First Colonial" was facing the "Green Run Stallions" for the year's first home game. Bradford was never big on sports but Larry being FC's quarterback, definitely ensured he never would. Everyone knew the finest girls from both schools, and a few colleges would be at the game, and so would he.

"Hey Brad, I thought that was you. Our family summer vacation ran a few weeks past the first day of school so I couldn't miss the first game. I've been so swamped with makeup homework, and taking notes, that I haven't had time for myself. I rode with a few of my girls after they convinced me tonight's episode of the Fresh Prince of Bel-Air would come on again, and that plenty of cute guys would be here, 'cause I'm not a school pep-rally supporter or sports person. So how was your summer, who you here with, and how many numbers you got so far? Don't lie either," Nicole added with a smile.

"I'm here by myself. All these girls is stuck up like any other girls. Summer was hectic, work, work, and mo work. Now I know why I never heard from you but you could have sent a postcard or something."

"No, I couldn't. All my girl cousins are nosey, my boy cousins are overprotective,my grandma is both, and what you mean stuck up like any other girls? What you saying? I know you ain't still on me about not sneaking you in my house to do the nasty! I told you I wasn't ready for all that, besides, you ain't even my boyfriend."

"Nah, that wasn't what I was saying. This is a new year, new school, I ain't thinking about having sex with you... Like you said, you ain't ready for all that."

"Oh yeah, you ain't thinking about it, huh? You got your haircut all tight, fresh from head to toe, rope chain on, L.L. Cool J's new tape in your walkman at a game full of girls lining the bleachers, and you ain't thinking about getting some?"

"Nope."

"Liar."

*

The freshly painted Black Cherry 1988 Mustang 5.0 was sitting on chrome rims, two Kicker 15" speakers on a Phoenix Gold amp, and dark tint on the windows.

"Hi Brad," the computer simulated voice of the Viper car alarm announced as he disarmed it before he and Nicole got inside.

"You know dem girls you was wit are a prime example of the stuck up girls I was talking bout right?" Bradford couldn't resist informing her.

"What you doing knowing if they stuck up or not? You just nasty? Matter of fact, who else been in this car before we go anywhere, Brad?" Nicole swung around and faced him for an answer with both arms folded across her ample chest.

Bradford loved her feistiness. Her attractive eyes narrowed while her nostrils flared in the silence allowed for his response. Nicole wore a finger wave hairstyle with a slight blonde dye that complimented her skin tone perfectly. Instead of answering the question, he pushed a Bell, Biv, Devoe tape in the tape deck and pulled out. "That girl is poison, never trust a big butt and a smile," blared from the speakers.

*

The Macthrift motel was two brick buildings with two floors divided by a parking lot. These buildings sat between 21ˢᵗ and 22ⁿᵈ Street, two blocks from Virginia Beach's oceanfront. Efficiency rooms were rented for $22.95 a day during the off season so Bradford used a fake I.D. to rent one after buying groceries from the Safeway grocery store a few blocks away.

"How did you know about this place? You took some chick here before, and why does it look like my grandma decorated everything?" Nicole asked while looking around, and barely sitting on the edge of one of the twin beds.

"My homeboy's mom is a maid here...You'll have to call the front desk about the carpets, blankets, and curtains. Old as the desk clerk is, she might have had some say in it, any more questions?" he asked with a smile while he unpacked the few bags of groceries.

"Uh huh. Hurry up and come over here to keep me warm, that heater blowing cold air," Nicole whined in a sexy drawl.

"Be right there, oh, and that wasn't a question."

After a last minute choice to order Dominos Pizza, instead of Pizza Hut, or cooked food, Bradford finally surrendered to the distant thought that things were not going to go as planned. Especially when Nicole climbed into the bed opposite the one he was in, fully dressed. He knew it was only a matter of time before she undressed because the heater had raised the temperature in the room too high for clothes and a blanket.

"I'm about to take a shower. I didn't plan this so my clothes are over at my girlfriend's... you know you need to take me by there to get them tomorrow, right?" Nicole said in a flirtatious tone before disappearing behind the bathroom door. Anticipation mixed with the unknown possibilities caused Bradford to experience huge butterflies all around the inside of his stomach. He got up off the bed and placed Keith Sweat's "Make it Last Forever" tape into the small portable Sony radio he'd brought upstairs. Then he made sure the room was dark except for the small stream of light slipping from between the bathroom door jamb. Bradford quietly walked over to the door and peeked inside. Nicole's naked silhouette could only be seen going through the showering motions behind the thick plastic multicolored shower curtain. Suddenly the curtain slid back and she stepped out of the shower fully lathered and grabbed a small bottle of complementary shampoo before darting back into the warmth of the shower's steam and closing the curtain. Nicole made eye contact with Bradford, redirected the showerhead to prevent the floor from getting wet, then pulled the curtain all the way open.

Bradford darted away from the door, heart racing, hoping she hadn't seen him. Unable to resist having another peek at her naked body, he returned to his position and immediately locked eyes with Nicole as she slowly caressed each breast in a sensual manner. She finished drying off while Bradford watched until she moved toward the bathroom door.

"Bradley, can you put some lotion on my back?" Nicole asked in a playful manner as she now sat on the bed and allowed the towel wrapped around her body to drop on the floor before climbing into bed and lying on her stomach.

Bradford knew she was naked underneath the covers. He also paid attention to the fact that she was now in his bed instead of the one on the other side of the room. He straddled her body just below her ass, before gently rolling back the covers and squirting lotion across her upper, and lower back.

"Damn boy, it's cold. Hurry up," Nicole said as she flinched.

He rubbed both hands together before skillfully massaging the lotion into her soft skin as she moaned softly. His hands worked slowly across her butt and stroked between her legs.

"Ummmm.... What do you think you're doing? I thought you said you weren't thinking about having sex with me?" Nicole said breathlessly, in small pants as she enjoyed the feeling of his fingers exploring her.

"I'm not," was all his brain could come up with in the heat of the moment.

"Uhh....You lie. If you weren't thinking about it why were you watching me through the door taking a shower?" she asked before turning over to face him while pulling the covers up to her neck.

"Same reason if you weren't ready, why you let me watch?" Bradford replied while skillfully easing the covers down her waist, exploring two round perky breasts.

"Okay Bradley, you have to be my boyfriend, not that part-time stuff all my girls be going through with guys."

"Cool," Bradford said before slipping his tongue into her mouth while Keith Sweat helped set the mood.

"You got a condom?" Nicole asked between moans as Bradford softly kissed her breast.

"Ummm hmmm," Bradford responded with one nipple in his mouth while caressing the other. He could feel Nicole's hands on the back of his head, as he worked his way a little past her navel and stopped.

Nicole's heavy breathing also came to an abrupt halt. "Why you stop? Keep going," she whined while parting her legs to give him a full frontal view.

Although the darkness prevented Bradford from seeing anything, he felt her legs open, and her hands trying to push him between them. "Whoa ...I don't eat no pussy."

"Damn, boy. You had to say it like that ? It was feeling sooo good! You got my legs shaking and shit. Feel how wet you got me down there."

Bradford slid out of his clothes and into a Trojan condom that he couldn't believe would finally be used. Especially on her, the girl of his dreams. He ran his hand along her inner thigh and felt both her warmth and extreme wetness as her legs trembled. After fumbling, poking, and probing he felt her hand guide him.

"Slow down and be gentle... It's my first time," Nicole moaned in his ear before wrapping her legs around his waist and squeezing to absorb the pain.

Bradford could feel her body tense up with each stroke. He noticed that the more he kissed on her neck and ears, the more her body relaxed. Soon Nicole's pelvic thrusts were swallowing him and demanding more. "Let me ride you," she said while easing from beneath him. Nicole climbed on top of him. She pulled his arm around her and snuggled as far into him as possible. Her heavy breathing quickly turned into soft snores.

CHAPTER FIVE

THE SMITH'S RESIDENCE WAS A tiny half bricked, half white vinyl siding ranch style house with black shingles and shutters. The small quaint home had three bedrooms, one bath and a waist high chain link fence that secured the sparsely growing patches of grass the owner obsessed over. The house was built one block away from interstate 264 which became a convenience and annoyance at the same time.

"That boy here for ya, I don't know what you see in him. I tell you, back in my day, a young man came and met your parents. That was called courting."

"Grandma, you said he couldn't come to your house because he lives in Atlantis, remember?" Nicole replied.

"You sure I said that, baby? You know your aunt and cousins stay there too? Anyway, tell that boy to come on in here so I can lay my eyes on 'em. Much as you go on bout 'em, I feel like I've known the boy all my life," Gertrude said bluntly. Nicole reluctantly stood in the doorway and motioned for Bradford to come inside with an obvious uneasy look.

"Come in, my grandma wants to meet you."

Bradford slowly approached the house that he'd been trying to persuade Nicole to sneak him inside for months. Now that he was invited, the desire to go inside was replaced with apprehension.

"Grandma, this is Bradley, Bradley, my grandma." Nicole spat out with a mix of nervousness and anxiety.

"Hello, Miss Smith. Pleased to meet you. By the way, I prefer being called Brad if you don't mind," Bradford said respectfully.

"Pleased to finally meet you as well, and call me Gerddy. Don't mind Nicole, she has a problem with calling people what she wants instead of the name you give her. But don't just stand there, have a seat. You'll have to excuse my house, it's such a mess. Would you care for something to eat or drink?" Gertrude asked with a girly tone that took Nicole completely by surprise.

"No thanks. Your home is lovely by the way, Miss Smith. I mean Gerddy. How do you deal with the regular, and tourism traffic that zooms up and down the interstate just a block away from your bedroom window?" Bradford asked out of a mixture of curiosity and being a little uncomfortable.

"I reckon the same way up yonder dem folks deal with those planes flying over Oceana... You adjust. So what are your plans for the future? My granddaughter seems to be quite fond of you."

"Grandma! You don't have to answer that. I can't believe you just said that... Let's go Brad," Nicole said while pulling him to his feet.

Bradford found himself being ushered out of the house and into the passenger seat of his own car. He watched nervously as Nicole rounded the front of the car before opening the driver side door and sitting beside him.

"So where is this place Superstars, and what do you need to go there for? You supposed to be spending the whole day with me not making stops," Nicole said with a playful smile, and hint of seriousness while adjusting the rear view mirror, before backing out of the gravel in front of her house.

"Girl, just drive. I know this is your day. You better be glad I'm letting you drive my baby. Take the interstate to Norfolk and get off on the Norfolk State exit. I'll tell you the rest when we get there," Bradford said while rifling through the glove box filled with tapes until he found "Naughty by Nature."

"Uh Uh. We ain't listening to no O.P.P. today. I'm driving, put in that Mary J Blige "Real Love" or Jodeci "Come and talk to me," Nicole said before making a left onto Granby Street as instructed and cruising along the one lane street that accommodated parked cars with meters, leaving just enough space between passing cars, and causing them to veer into oncoming traffic with the same limited spacing. "Why are the lanes so small? You have to cross the middle double lines to pass the park cars."

"Well, you wanted to drive, so drive. Make sure you stop for those cars. Don't just pull into their lane. If they stop and wait for you to go, then go," Bradford said as tension in his body began to ease when the specific building they were heading to came into view.

Presumptuous

The chimes in the doorway alerted whoever was working that customers had entered the establishment. This was especially necessary because the majority of the operation was performed in the back behind a thick dark curtain. Superstar's glass display case ran a few feet away from the far-right wall, and made a left at the end of the left wall. This display case was lined with charms, necklaces, bracelets, earrings, designer pieces, birthstones, specialty pieces, and gold teeth. The display of gold teeth consisted of a velvet display filled with gold shaped individual teeth with openings on each side. These could be found in corner stores, Chinese owned stores, and mall kiosks. The problem was these teeth were constantly being tried on by customers. Aside from sanitary issues, it was only a matter of time before the thin metal would lose its grip on the tooth. This quality matched the price of $15.

Superstars designed the style, along with the number of teeth requested. This was commonly called a "bridge," and ranged from $350 to $700.

"What's up, Jake?" Bradford spoke with an air of assurance and cockiness as he strolled past the crowd of guys leaning over a section of the display counter while pointing at the large display case hanging on the wall behind the counter. Nicole noticed the sudden change in Bradford but brushed it off as some male thing she couldn't possibly understand, before browsing the section of the case closest to the door.

Bradford tried on his teeth but was more interested in the group of guys making their way towards Nicole. He could see them pretending to look at jewelry and sliding closer to her through the small mirror used to check out customer's purchases. "Come here, baby, tell me what you think," Bradford said as a quick solution.

Nicole's concentration on the ring that caught her eye was being interrupted for the second time since she entered the store. The first time one of the guys in the store kept whispering pssst until she looked up to see a mouth full of ridiculous gold teeth, and a long chain holding a charm with a man and woman having sex. Nicole rolled her eyes and returned her attention to a cluster of diamonds that would look much better on her hand than the display case she was looking through.

"Yes baby," she answered in a sweet sexy voice that made it obvious she wanted something before sashaying past a group of admirers, and enjoying the attention.

"What you think?" Bradford asked as Nicole stood before him with an expression on her face that he couldn't read.

"Uh.... nice, baby, it looks nice. Come see this ring I want," Nicole quickly said while rushing Bradford towards the display section where her desire rested.

"Let me get that too. I know you're going to look out on the price," Bradford said with confidence as he watched Nicole's eyes sparkle more than the cluster she was currently trying on while Jake produced a decorative ring box.

Nicole had been relieved of her driving position as soon as they left Superstars. She sat silently and thought of how stupid the guy looked inside with the gold teeth and chain. Not only had Bradford purchased a mouth full of gold, his chain and charm depicted a man and woman having sex doggy style with diamonds representing cum. There was no way her grandmother could see any of that. Nicole was watching the power of jewelry transform Bradford's attitude and swagger right before her very eyes as he hung out the window and beeped the horn at people he barely knew while smiling, and exposing every gold tooth his lips permitted.

The next stop was Military Circle Mall which was where Nicole had planned to spend a portion of their day anyway, before the hour long stop to Superstars. They walked casually, holding hands while Nicole made sure her cluster, and the fact that they were hand-in-hand, stood out to any females who noticed the gold, and diamonds around his neck, and in his mouth.

McCory's was a department store in the mall that only Military Circle Mall had. Everybody came to buy the clip-on gold teeth found in a display case at the front of the store. Gold name plates twisted in cursive, t-shirts and clothes airbrushed by a few guys called the "Shirt Kings," or to take pictures in front of the airbrushed mural. Bradford paid for two stonewashed Guess Jean jumpers that were dropped off a week in advance to be airbrushed. Nicole didn't know which surprised her more, the fact that he knew her size, or her name and his name airbrush in graffiti down the front, and back of each pant leg with a picture of their faces on the front. After they both changed into white t-shirts, white Air Force 1 Nikes, and the airbrushed jumpers, Bradford placed a gold name plated necklace around her neck that spelled out Bradford and Nicole forever.

The mural had Bugs Bunny standing in front of a red Mercedes Benz convertible with two gold crowns around his front teeth, a beeper on his waist while he talked on his cell phone, and Scooby-Doo sitting behind the steering wheel, with a big chain around his neck holding his initials in a charm.

The food court in the mall was packed with a variety of fast food counters, cultural establishments, and employees offering free sample dishes to hungry shoppers. The lines were so long at the usual fast food chain counters that they opted for Chinese food.

"Brad, I love my necklace and my ring," Nicole gushed while making sure not to get any of the reddish-orange General Tso's chicken sauce from her fingers on her outfit.

"I'm glad I was able to detour, and still make your day at the same time," Bradford replied while looking over the pictures they took.

Nicole instantly detected the sarcastic undertone although there was none in his voice or body expression, she knew the words were carefully chosen. "Okay, okay... Maybe your little stops were not that bad. I wanted to catch a movie but maybe I can make a little stop too?" Nicole said with a devilish grin. They both left the mall parking lot with Nicole behind the wheel, headed to The Atrium Hotel in Virginia Beach.

CHAPTER SIX

2001

"GOOD MORNING LADIES AND GENTLEMEN. My name is Professor Strickland. Welcome to real estate abstracting," the small Asian man wearing a brown tweed sports jacket, jeans, brown boots, and maroon bow tie, said as he wrote his name in chalk with remarkable penmanship across the massive blackboard. "This semester we will be covering abstracting titles, recordation of land transactions, liens, and covenants. Class, please take out your textbooks and read chapters one through five. For homework, I'm handing out review sheets on these five chapters."

Full academic scholarship meant taking a lot of notes, several study halls, extra credit assignments, cramming, missing homecoming games and frat parties to maintain a 3.0 GPA. Even with these hurdles, Bradford maintained a 3.8 GPA. It seemed like yesterday Professor Strickland introduced himself. Now that the semester was over and spring break was near, he questioned if he wanted to continue studying law, or if returning next semester was even what he wanted to do.

At fifty-four years old, Monica Williams had beaten the odds. As a single parent and widower, she raised a son that finished school, lived past the average lifespan of a young black male, and had never been subjected to any run-ins with the judicial system. She put herself through college and became a registered nurse. The endless twelve-hour shifts scheduled over the last 10 years allowed her the ability to pay a bank mortgage for a 3-bedroom, two-and-a-half bath with garage in an upper-middle-class subdivision on time. Monica was medium built but shapely, five foot even, with a short bob haircut, dark brown eyes, and smooth hazelnut hued skin. Her life was structured and her approach thorough and serious since her late husband's death. Now that wisdom had set in with age she regretted a lot of decisions made, especially when they were pertaining to her only son. A wedge had been driven between the two of them so long ago that the knowledge of how, when, and why was surely as elusive and mind-boggling for him as it was for her. Monica prayed fervently every night that God would somehow restore their relationship.

"Ma... Hey Ma, you home?" Bradford shouted, announcing his presence as he entered her house making sure she had enough time to make herself presentable if need be. He carried luggage into the guest room and found clean sheets on the bed with towels and wash clothes folded on top.

"I'm here, son. I'm in the kitchen warming up some leftovers. Will you have some?"

"Depends... what is it?" Monica hated it when he asked that question. Usually her response would be food!! She didn't want to fight, make him uncomfortable, or run him away so she went against her norm. "Chinese takeout."

"Sounds good, what are you doing home? You're usually working around this time." He knew this and tried to avoid her.

"I swapped shifts with a girlfriend of mine so I could go grocery shopping, get the other car serviced, and do a little laundry to prepare for your stay," she said with a smile.

"I told you not to make a big fuss over me coming home."

"I know, I know. I'm just glad to see you here. It's mighty lonely in this house by myself all the time. Feels good to have you home, baby," she said before hugging and placing a warm kiss on each of his cheeks. "How's school?"

"Okay, I guess, no complaints."

"I see... Guess who I ran into at the hospital earlier today?"

"Who?" Bradford asked.

"Sabrina. You do remember Sabrina, don't you? She was supposed to be my daughter-in-law and give me a couple grandbabies," Monica said with hopeful eyes that scanned her son's face for any hidden feelings given away by body language.

"I remember Sabrina, Mom, how is she?"

"Well, she goes to school out there near you. The rest you can find out for yourself. Here is her number. She said to give it to you."

"How she look?" Bradford asked with a sly grin after conceding to the trap his mother had obviously set.

"Boy, I told you to call her. That's all I'm saying. My lips are sealed... Better yet, my mouth is full," Monica said in a playful tone before placing a spoonful of beef and broccoli in her mouth and smiling innocently at the whole ordeal.

"I'll call her after I eat, okay?" Bradford said before eating and falling fast asleep from exhaustion.

*

"Mmm.... something smells good," Bradford said as he inhaled the aroma of a full breakfast that included sausage, eggs, buttermilk pancakes, grapefruit, and freshly squeezed orange juice. He surveyed the kitchen before sitting at the table wrapped in a towel. After enjoying a good breakfast he cleaned the table, then it hit him... One of many vicious flashbacks.

Flashback ....

"Bradford! Come here this instant. These dishes look clean to you?! Look at those water stains. Boy, get in there and wash every dish in the dish rack again!"

Tears weighed down the rim of each eyelid as he thoroughly inspected each dish out of habit, refusing to surrender one more drop of pain from his eyes. "I've got to get out of here," he concluded before leaving the rest of the dishes in the sink out of anger, hurt, and spite.

*

The garage concealed a midnight blue 2000 Lincoln Navigator that his mother had recently purchased along with a 2001 midnight blue Lincoln LS Sedan as a package deal. Each vehicle was a fully loaded edition. Bradford's late arrival didn't give him enough time to settle in and check out the LS in the daylight, and he knew Monica had probably gone to work before he woke up.

*

"Customer needs a sales associate in electronics," someone announced throughout the Kmart building. Bradford heard the summoning of someone who could unlock the glass display case filled with Xbox 360 games, particularly Fight Night, Call of Duty, and John Madden football.

"Excuse me sir, how can I help you?"

Bradford continued to browse through music CDs without turning around. He half turned his head and spoke over his left shoulder. "Let me get Madden, Fight Night, and Call of Duty, and I'm going to grab a few CDs real quick."

"Bradford, is that you? How long you been back, and when were you going to let me know?" Nicole asked with obvious hurt in her voice, overpowering the initial surprise on her face.

"I just got back last night as a matter of fact. How have you been?"

"Mmm hmmm. That'll be one-ninety-five. Will it be cash or credit?" she asked after twisting her mouth to one side, signaling she didn't believe he just returned last night.

"I'm not a math major but I know my total should have been more than that... I wouldn't want to get you in any sort of trouble."

"I gave you my employee discount, silly. You don't deserve it anyway."

"Well, what time you get off? I'm thinking maybe we can do a little catching up. Or maybe not," Bradford answered his own question after seeing her body language signal an internal struggle. "Thanks, take care, and it was nice bumping into you," Bradford said before taking the plastic bags from her hand and walking away.

Nicole stood there stunned. A wave of emotions ranging from anger, hurt, disappointment, and fear consumed every inch of her being. She quickly tried to regroup and sort through cloudy judgment before a mistake was made that she might regret for the rest of her life. Nicole sprinted through the automatic front doors straight into the parking lot and made a quick scan before finding her target "Hey.. give.. give me... ah... minute to clock out... and I'll be.... right back," she squeezed out between gasps after knocking on the passenger side window of the dark blue Navigator.

Before Bradford could respond, he was watching the red and black Kmart uniform running in the opposite direction, and he enjoyed every second of the bounce and jiggle she showed him.

*

"You're mighty quiet over there. I know you're not shy or nervous around me. Looks like you might have come home with the gold if you had tried out for the Olympics the way you came across that parking lot," Bradford teased.

"Ha ha," Nicole said before sticking her tongue out, then smiling. "So where we going? What's up wit you? Got a girlfriend? How long you back? You said you want to catch up, right?" Nicole asked without expression or a clue as to her feelings, or position on each line of questioning.

"I know where this is going… see Nik... I didn't tell you I was accepted to Georgetown because being apart from you was going to be hard enough without arguing about it, then having to see your face while saying goodbye. It would have been too much. I'm sorry if I hurt you. There's no girlfriend. I'm back for spring break. Not much is going on since we last saw each other except my missing you and we can go wherever you like," Bradford explained with deep sincerity.

"I have an idea, go by my house so I can grab some clothes. You do remember where I live, right? Don't call me Nik either, you haven't earned that right back yet, I hate when you call me that."

Bradford waited outside her grandmother's house while she ran in and came out with a black tote bag. The ride to his mom's house was quiet except for the butterflies flipping around vigorously in each of their stomachs. As soon as the automatic garage door opener was pressed Nicole exited the truck and went inside.

*

"Yo Nik, where you disappear to...where you at?"

"Oh my goodness, that shower was just what I needed. The temperature was perfect and the shower head... Let's just say after a long day of work I know where your mother can't wait to get to," Nicole teased while drying her hair.

"Now that you've given me that disturbing image, I'll have to start using the other shower. Thanks a lot, Nik. Come on downstairs after you get yourself together. I know I didn't stop by your house long but my mom should have something in there you can fit," Bradford said.

Nicole entered the dining room wearing a pair of navy blue cotton thong panties and one of his long gray Georgetown Hoyas t-shirt. Bradford instantly noticed her perky nipples pressing aggressively against the fabric. She wore her hair pulled back in a ponytail. "What is all this? Candlelight, lobster tail, asparagus, dinner rolls, and white wine too? Went all out, didn't cha? I hope you ain't do all this thinking you gone get some?" Nicole said before being seated by Bradford.

"Nah. You're special and it's a must that you are always treated as such... No expense spared."

"Mmm hmm," Nicole responded while nibbling on a piece of asparagus and eyeing him untrustingly.

*

Their lips touched with delicate gentleness while both of their tongues met with deep urgency. Maxwell could be heard singing "This Woman's Work" from speakers that were hidden somewhere in the room, set to a low volume, so it seemed like a soundtrack to their love making in Nicole's mind.

"Bradley. We really shouldn't be doing this.... Why you gotta do this to me," she whined as he ran each finger along her naked body before placing an index finger against her lips to quiet her.

"Just relax and allow your body to give in."

Their bodies entangled, rolling back and forth. Bradford entered her with patience while staring into her eyes. Each stroke was met with an even push back.

"Why didn't you use a rubber, baby?" Nicole moaned in between heavy panting. The question was only asked so if she happened to get pregnant it could be revisited, making him, and only him, at fault in her mind. Their reunion lasted all night long, as every position and explorations of all five senses were met. Afterwards, they fell into a deep sleep in each other's arms.

CHAPTER SEVEN

2014

"AGAIN, I APOLOGIZE FOR THE turbulence, sir." The captain's voice sounded worried coming across the intercom system.

The passenger and company were not only precious cargo, he owned the private jet held together with rivets that were currently being tested by nature. The owner, Bradford Williams the Third, took deep breaths to calm his fear of heights. His mind was preoccupied with his hair constantly thinning that resulted in a brash decision to shave it all off and wear it bald before the sudden interruption of turbulence. Both pedicured bare feet tensed up, then relaxed by stretching and retracting all ten toes simultaneously. He loosened the royal blue tie around his neck, removed both platinum cufflinks, then returned to the unfamiliar feeling of rubbing his newly shaven bald head. Aging was an issue money could not stop, though many had countless surgical procedures trying to show that it could. Bradford opted for the young, clean-shaven face, plenty of H2O, balanced meals, exercise, at least 8 hours of sleep and a spiritual balance that was badly in need of work. "Remind me again why I am doing this?" he asked the lovely blonde sitting next to him wearing a skin-tight business suit.

"Tax write-off. Your accountant reported an amount that legally has to be paid to the government. This transitions into your give-back campaign, should you choose to buy into the political endorsements and one day run for office. Now, we will be landing soon. A bulletproof Range Rover HSE model will pick us up. The driver was handpicked as an expert in hand-to-hand combat, retired CIA, with excellent marksmanship credentials. Your timeshare unit at the Barclay Tower Turtle Kay has been warmed to your specific requirements. Will there be anything else I can do for you, sir?" The blonde temp service replacement for his personal assistant of over 15 years asked with enthusiasm.

Bradford raised his head slightly from the recliner position of the seat while readjusting his tie. "I will be needing adequate companionship. Two, maybe 3 escorts. Submissive, shoulder length hair, slight tan, well-traveled, with an athletic build, and no inhibitions. Non-negotiable."

"I'll get right on it, Mr. Williams," she said with a pleasant smile as the wheels of the plane began braking on the tarmac of the private landing strip.

"Enjoy your flight, Mr. Williams?" The six-foot-two bodyguard asked as he held the rear door of the SUV open.

"No small talk. You're employed to drive. Let's not broach this subject again or I'll have you replaced at the next intersection," Bradford said without lifting his eyes from the information scrolling across his BlackBerry cellphone screen.

The airtight cabin conducted a smooth yet soothing mixture of tire rotation with a slight hint of transmission changing of gears. Bradford was impressed with the fact that he had to look over the driver's shoulder once or twice to observe the RPM needle rise and fall.

"I found a reputable firm, sir," the assistant said. "I sent a few prospects to your phone. The different time zones may present a slight problem but we shouldn't have a problem circumventing this. The urgency of service and promise of repeat business with heavy tipping should take care of any hang-ups,"

He smiled at her ability to be discreet, then thumbed through the beautiful choices she sent to his phone. "Driver, I seem to recall a few of you CIA boys getting into trouble overseas behind a breach in security involving escorts not being paid? Might you have any expertise in this particular area?"

With the hint of a smile in the driver's voice, he simply replied, "In fact, I do. That will not be a problem. Will you be needing anything else, sir?"

"See, that little incident has proven to be beneficial to us both. God, I love this country!" Bradford announced, before sipping a bottle of Fuji spring water as they safely arrived at their destination.

Philanthropy

The auditorium was filled with inquisitive, yet impressionable young minds. He was still digesting the size of the enormous parking lot that wrapped around the newly built brick building he now stood in. The long, thick curtains he stood behind didn't shield him from the large overhead spotlights that seemed to be playing heat ping-pong with the lights mounted at the foot of the stage, and the maple syrup colored wood flooring.

"Without further ado, I bring you Bradford Williams III. Let's give him a warm welcoming round of applause," a voice intoned from the other side of the curtains.

Bradford appeared with both hands above his head, turning them in a quick motion at the wrist. "Please be seated," he implored before gently placing his hands on the podium. Once he adjusted the flexible microphone he began. "Yes, you sir, third row from the front in the red jacket."

"Where you from, and what you do.I ain't never seen or heard of you?"

"I see, tough crowd," Bradford said with a smile that was met with laughter by the adults in the room. "I'm from here, actually; I grew up in Atlantis apartments with some of your parents, no doubt. When I was going to elementary school it was the "Old Seatack" the police now use for training across the street from the McDonalds on Birdneck Road. I'm sure you've all seen the huge charter buses that go to Kings Dominion and Bush Gardens every summer. That's my company that sponsors the trip."

The crowd's excitement signaled that at least a few of the students in attendance enjoyed those events themselves. An unusual, yet delightful feeling had taken over since he reached the area but he would never let on, nor admit it, even to himself. Home always had some effect on the mind, no matter who you were. Bradford used his money, power, and influence to remove himself from any association he had with Virginia Beach, Virginia. It was a reminder of poverty, racism,an unjust judicial system that mandated jury for certain crimes,sadness, and struggle. He had no real voice here, everywhere else in the world, he was the voice.

"You a sellout. You ain't from Lantis. You better not get caught out there by yourself!"

The sudden outburst awoke an aggressive demeanor he no longer thought he had. Bradford became deeply offended when he knew he shouldn't have. Was he proud to be seen as a stranger... or was he? "That's all the time I have for questions. I'd like to thank you all for having me," he said before waving and exiting behind the curtains, with his driver keeping pace. They made their way down the hallway to the exit where the driver left Bradford standing on the sidewalk while he pulled the truck around.

"You were great in there," the assistant said after the clicking sound of her heels stopped.

"Mr. Williams, Mr. Williams, please wait for a minute!" Bradford ignored the young, female voice beckoning him as he was escorted to the rear seat of the vehicle. The young, persistent student walked calmly around to his window and tapped lightly.

Thirty minutes later...

The Range Rover made a smooth transition from the school parking lot onto the newly paved Birdneck Road. Bradford leaned against the door, second guessing the "spur of the moment" decision he had just made. She seemed too relaxed and sure of herself at such a young age, which could only mean trouble. Bradford studied her almond-shaped eyes, smooth caramel skin, and somehow vaguely familiar pointy nose. Her long, black, silky hair was pulled back into a ponytail with short bangs hanging in front.

"Now, young lady, you say you have every letter I've ever written, and your mother has started a 529 college fund with money sent by me every month, correct?"

"Yes, sir. Because of you, I will be able to attend the college of my choosing, assuming my grades allow my acceptance," she replied with confidence.

"Mary Nicole Smith… and your mother's name is Nicole Smith? You could be her, twenty or so years ago… The resemblance is uncanny," Bradford said. He knew Sabrina, his personal assistant, who was now conveniently on vacation, was responsible for this whole ordeal somehow. Sabrina grew up with him and stayed in contact with the old neighborhood. He had to speak to her about giving his money to everyone who produced a heartbreaking story of the past; it seemed he overlooked a major one. Bradford was very interested in meeting the conniving woman he remembered as being so sweet and endearing. This scheme had clearly amassed a substantial amount of money, which he feared might require legal advice, and bringing in the proper authorities.

ATL

The right turn into Atlantis Apartments created instant nostalgia as the truck skipped at the same part of the road his mother Monica's blue Nova always did returning home from some outing as a child. The red brick apartment buildings had half faced bricks sticking out in a rock climbing wall type formation. Each building had three or four hallways with four apartments found in each one. The grass was manicured, the bushes trimmed, and the trees properly mulched and pruned. The black asphalt was recently painted with bold white lines that showed apartment numbers, or the word, "visitor." A large, dark brown painted dumpster, with sliding doors on each side, sat surrounded by weather treated wooden fencing in every court. An occasional police car could be seen parked, awaiting some reason to stop a suspicious motorist or pedestrian.

*

Bradford instantly took notice of the mint green floral pattern obviously painted on the living room's white walls with a stenciled roller of some sort. Great time and effort had been put into choosing the colors, including a warm, welcoming canary-yellow used in the dining room. He slowly removed the designer suit jacket he was wearing and placed it beside the assistant who sat attentively on a white suede sectional couch. Bradford walked around the room carefully looking at pictures, figurines, plants and other decorations to get a better feel of what kind of monster he was about to face.

"That's you and my mom in fifth grade," Mary pointed out in a class picture sitting on a bookcase on her way out of the room. She returned with a stack of letters wrapped in rubber bands. He skimmed over a few and saw his signature stamped at the closing of each item in question.

"May I use your lavatory?" Bradford asked after handing back the stack of letters and concealing a few for evidence.

"Sure. You know the way, right? Where's my manners? Would either of you like something to eat or drink?" Mary offered her guests.

"No, thank you. We will be grabbing something to eat once I leave here. Wouldn't want to spoil our appetites," Bradford spoke from the bathroom.

"Mary, did you see which of them fast tail girl's house the drug dealer driving that expensive truck went into? They parked in my damn parking space again! Cost me three years of paychecks to drive something like that around," Nicole said, preoccupied with the front door deadbolt and an arm full of groceries.

"Oh, I'm sorry, didn't see you there. You must be from the school? I'm Mary's mother, Nicole. Just what has she done to make you stop by so late?" asked Nicole, giving Mary a stern look while shaking the hand of the blonde, white woman, dressed in a navy blue pinstriped pantsuit, sitting with perfect posture on her couch.

"Uh...no.. ma'am, I'm sorry for the mix-up. I'm here-"

"With me. I apologize for taking your parking space. By the way, I am not a drug dealer. Though I do business with a few pharmaceutical conglomerates, if that counts," Bradford interrupted while meticulously drying each hand with one of the expensive, decorative, mint green hand towels that unbeknownst to him were forbidden to be used. He was instantly caught in a trance, and a feeling of emotional uncertainty as soon as his eyes left his hands and met hers.

"Oh my God... Brad, is that you?" was all Nicole could convince her brain to come up with, and her mouth to say. Her pulse quickened and they were back in time, in love again, just like that in her mind.

CHAPTER EIGHT

"LORD, I WANT TO THANK you for allowing me to see one more day. You said you wouldn't place anymore on us than we can bear. Thank you for the unexpected visitor... work those issues out for each and every one of us. I ask that you give me the strength to do your will in the name of the Father, Son, and precious Holy Ghost. In Jesus name, I pray..... Amen." Nicole slowly got off both knees with wet stains on her pearl white slip and teardrops still streaming down her cheeks. A small women's stainless steel Citizen watch wrapped around her left wrist read five in the morning. She quickly showered then wrapped a mint green towel around her body, overlapped both ends with a fold over the top of each breast. This particular towel was for decoration only but since Bradford used it, she decided it now belonged in the linen closet with the rest of the usable towels. She was a stickler for things being in their respective places. A conversation about the towel was all but inevitable. Nicole used the palm of her hand to wipe the steam from the bathroom mirror. The door was cracked once the mirror continued to keep fogging up. After brushing her teeth in her usual way that would have bordered on erotic had some male been present, she daintly opened the towel and examined her glistening nakedness.

At forty-three, Nicole's body showed no physical evidence of having had a thirteen-year-old daughter that slept peacefully in a bedroom next door to her bedroom. Nicole searched her own almond shaped eyes, smooth caramel skin, and perfect short button nose that differed from her daughters. The dormant past was now very much active.... explaining this would not be easy. Suddenly Nicole felt invigorated. She sat on the edge of the tub and removed her old clear coat toenail polish before applying a fresh coat of Fire Engine Red, instead of her usual favorite, safe Mint Green. After removing the towel wrapped around her long shiny black hair with blonde streaks, she gently blow dried it on a low speed so as to not disturb her daughter's rest. She returned to her room, walking on both heels in order to prevent each toenail from smearing. She laid out red lacy Victoria Secret silk panties and a matching bra. In doing so she felt totally exhilarated. Nicole straightened everything before preparing breakfast and waking her baby up for school. "Time to get up, sleepy head," Nicole whispered while lightly shaking her daughter.

"Okay, mom. I'm getting up already," Mary said before rolling over and pulling the covers back over her head to block the sun rays let in through the blinds. Ten minutes later she drug her small slim frame into the bathroom and stretched the corners of her mouth with each index finger to see her braces rubber bands in the mirror before brushing. In six months she felt the improvement more than she could see it. After her usual bathroom routine, Mary threw on a powder pink Baby Phat t-shirt, dark blue skinny jeans, and matching pink Converse All Star sneakers.

"Make sure you eat everything on that plate. Place those dishes in the sink and run water over them. I love you." Nicole said before kissing Mary and heading towards the front door.

"Ma, was you glad to see Brad?" Mary asked to soothe her curiosity.

"Were you,not was you?,and Mr. Brad, since you insist on Brad instead of Mr. Williams. I'd prefer you call him Mr. Williams. Now to answer your question... Yes, I suppose it was nice to see him. Why are you so concerned, young lady?"

"Oh... cause you never wear those panties."

Nicole blushed and headed out the door to prevent the conversation from carrying on any further. 'What am I doing, behaving like a little school girl over this man?' Nicole thought to herself as she started the vehicle. She had to laugh at her daughter's astute observation. Luckily the conversation had taken place in the privacy of their home and not in public. Either it was that obvious, Mary had gotten too comfortable, or she had been too careless with laying out her unmentionables across the bed without closing the door. Whatever the case, it would have to take a backseat to the countless other thoughts, potential issues, and decisions, starting with finding a parking space at the job, Seatack Community Center, where she worked as the head coordinator for the senior citizens.

"Hello, Gertrude, how are you this lovely morning?" Nicole asked after entering the building.

"Gerddy. You sure seem full of life all of a sudden; who is he and what's his name?" the eighty-year-old woman inquired without taking her eyes off the large knitting needles she was using.

"Now I see where my daughter gets that stubborn name thing from. You don't like mom, ma, or grandma... and I'm not calling you Gerddy or Gerttie... sounds so girlfriendish," Nicole said with a defiance aimed more towards one of the day's first decisions than the subject matter. "Tell me, when could I possibly have time for, or be interested in one?"

"Mmmmm, hmm... What name thing with my grandbaby are you going on about?" Gertrude chose to ask instead of continuing with the subject of her own name.

Nicole had begun busying herself when she decided to go ahead and get the situation over with early. "Brad's in town. He stopped by the house and we're having dinner tonight to catch up on old times.... He says to tell you hello.... there, you happy?" Nicole asked somewhat exhausted.

"I've always liked that boy, he come from stock,good people. I knew he'd be something even way back then."

"So why did you end up forbidding me to see him?" Nicole asked, shocked at what she was now hearing. She distinctly remembered her mother telling her she was glad her pregnancy wasn't by Bradford Williams, then going on further about how his mother raised him.

"That boy was trouble.... Not the usual kind all the other boys were. No. He had ambition, the kind that might destroy, or swallow up anything in its way. I just didn't want you to lose yourself in him," Gertrude revealed.

"Your influence and meddling caused so much hurt and uncertainty. Don't you think maybe you should have shared this little piece of information back then, at least when I told you he was going off to college?" Nicole asked, now overwhelmed by her mother's audacity.

Nicole's birth mother had been killed by her then boyfriend after she was born. Explaining the details always ended up being vague coming from her grandmother Gertrude who willingly took on the responsibility of raising her. Nicole always thought it best to obey her grandmother when it came to the opposite sex, overlooking the fact that each boy received the same warning as the one before. Bradford had become smitten with her, once the feelings were mutual a wedge was placed and driven by her grandma. This was not as clear then to her as it was this very moment. Nicole remembered hearing her grandmother crying many nights and asking God why he took her only daughter. She didn't want to cause her grandmother any further heartache by also disobeying relationship advice.

"I'm an old fool, child. Then I was a young fool. You have no idea what it's like to lose a child. God forbid you are ever forced to bear such a heavy burden. I was left with the task of raising and protecting you. I wasn't going to make the same mistake again. There was no such thing as godmothers, and all that other mess y'all young folks come up with nowadays. Your father went to prison for killing your mother and I wouldn't dare let his family get their filthy paws on you so they could poison your mind by taking you to see that animal. Maybe that wasn't the best thing to do but I was hurt and angry... He took my baby from me. I have made many mistakes. Bradford being one of many, and for that I'm truly sorry baby. What I won't apologize for is protecting you the best way I know how," Gertrude confessed with tears sliding down her barely wrinkled face.

"I forgive you. It's water under the bridge... whatever that means. I just wish I knew back then when I could have done something about it. I'm sure I'll be in similar shoes when my daughter is all grown up and reminding me of some scar left on her life, behind a decision made, that there was no way possible for me to know the long-lasting effects it would have in the future," Nicole explained with deep true understanding.

Apprehensive

Everything seemed to be going all wrong. At some point, Nicole had decided to call the whole thing off, except she forgot to get Bradford's cell phone number earlier so there was no way to contact him. "My favorite bottle of perfume is empty, the curiosity of Mary, no doubt." Nicole knew there wasn't enough time to stop by Lynnhaven Mall and pick up a new bottle from Macy's department store. She'd have to make do with the back up fragrances that were for school conferences, business meetings, or family gatherings. Nicole placed her French tipped nails of her pointer finger against the edge of her bottom row of teeth and slightly bit down as a gesture of indecisiveness. The white dinner dress hugged her like she needed to be held, firm and tight. "Not bad, not bad at all." The problem was her red panties could be seen and wearing a slip defeated the purpose of choosing a revealing dress. The black dress choice was just as satisfying but it would show her panty line and required the absence of a bra. Basically, she would be naked under the black choice, or wear the white one and have everyone know she was wearing red panties. The black one would massage her naked body all night which would be a change of pace from the usual "one on one" love sessions held in her room late night.

"Ma... Wear the black one. I like that one. You never wear it... since Mr. Larry," Mary said before thinking her words all the way through.

Nicole felt a sharp pain stab her body. Normally Mary would have been scolded for calling her father Larry, let alone Mr. Larry. They had been estranged, now separated for over a year now. Nicole knew the relationship was all wrong on so many levels from the beginning, but Mary came along so she tried to do the right thing in a wrong situation. Now he was neither seen nor heard from. Nicole understood that her daughter was too young to know or understand. Unable to be more shocked over the black ensemble, or that her daughter recalled Larry being the last recipient worthy of her fussing over, Nicole decided not to respond to either comment.

"My baby is growing up so fast. Now I need you to behave while I am gone and I'll bring you something back. Grandma is coming over and your butt should be asleep when I get back... Right?" Nicole asked, waiting for a response, knowing Mary thought she was too old for a babysitter.

"Right. Why can't I stay home by myself?" Mary replied while pouting with an innocent look on her face.

*

The Olive Garden on Lynnhaven Parkway was filled to capacity. After a thirty minute wait for a table, they were ushered over to a nice section where other customers were dining at a reasonable noise level.

"There's something about that dress. I'm not sure if it was made for you, or if you were made for it but you compliment each other well," Bradford charmingly admitted.

"I bet you say that to all the girls, Bradley... by the way, I'm sure it works too," Nicole interjected before they both enjoyed a good tension releasing laugh.

The server took both orders and returned with a bottle of white wine to sip while they waited.

"Not that I'm complaining, because we could have had Dominos extra cheese and black olives, which is a unique taste my grandma swears came from my mom's pregnancy cravings. Anyway... why did you choose here? I expected the red carpet treatment from you, sir," Nicole said, poking him with her finger in a playful manner.

"Well, I wanted to share this evening with regular people, embrace the nostalgia of being home. Enjoying your company, however brief, was my only thought and intention. We can always fly off the coast to some "fancy smancy" spot on a secluded island of your choice... right now in fact, if you'd like?"

"Naaaaaaaah," Nicole replied, emulating the character Lisa from the movie "Coming to America."

CHAPTER NINE

"SO, YOU REMEMBER MY MOM dragging me off the dance floor back then? And you find that funny? She beat me black and blue over trying to see you. The reason I missed school all the following weeks was swelling, not punishment. I swear if I'm ever blessed with having a child, I will never beat them," Bradford explained with sincerity.

"I'm sorry... I had no idea, Brad," Nicole said softly before gently placing her hand on his arm.

"Gotcha!" he said playfully.

"That's not funny, Brad. A lot of kids were abused back then and no one did anything about it," Nicole replied.

"I know, you're right. I'm sure I was one of them. I got my ass beat and punished that night... It was a different time and that's how things were done back then. The Bible scripture "Spare the rod, spoil the child," was taken too literally in some homes. My mother and I have never fully recovered from events like that from my childhood. I would have let my kid go to the dance in the first place."

"So, you agree with corporal punishment.... Is that what you're saying?" Nicole asked with her full attention being given, awaiting an answer.

"Okay, timeout. Maybe I'm not qualified to be speaking on corporal punishment, especially when you're getting all politically correct. We called it beatings. I know you have a daughter and I don't. This is a sensitive subject and I don't want to seem insensitive by any means. I will say whatever side you stand on obviously works for you because your daughter is quite the young lady," Bradford said with a warm smile.

"Mmmm....hmmm. That Georgetown law loophole shit don't work over here but that little compliment you slid in was nicely done," Nicole replied with a mouth full of food.

"Well, potty mouth, I hope you taught her to never talk with a mouth full," he said before they both had a good laugh. "While we're on the subject, care to explain to me why I am providing Mary with a full college education?" Bradford slipped in before cutting into the grilled chicken on his plate, then gently placing it on his tongue.

The room suddenly became tense. Nicole shifted slightly in her seat and flipped through a mental Rolodex of possible responses. After a quick gulp of wine, clearing her throat, and patting of the chest, Nicole responded, "Woo, something must have gone down the wrong pipe. It was an essay that she wrote for a contest she won."

Bradford sensed her unease as soon as the question was asked. He decided to leave the subject alone until more information was gathered. It was obvious something more was going on but he couldn't make sense of any other possibilities. "Happenstance is what happened earlier after my engagement. How else would I have met Mary, and reunited us? You should be very proud. I imagine she would win any contest that held her interest. If ever I've had the pleasure of meeting a contestant deserving of winning a college education, it's her. I don't understand why Sabrina didn't just give her a scholarship sponsored by my company, and offer a stipend once school started? I'll check on that when she returns from vacation. We do want our little star to have every advantage afforded to her," Bradford assured.

"How is Sabrina? I seem to recall you had a thing for her back in the day. Naturally, when you ran off to be a Georgetown Hoya and she happened to end up at Howard University, I expected little Brad to follow at some point," Nicole said to bait him into revealing the truth about the past.

"She's fine. She gets on my nerves but she's still the same old Brina. She's family, happily dating, as far as I know, but her personal affairs don't ever come up. In fact, she's been on me about the need to meet someone and settle down and have kids before it's too late. She means well. It's her constant badgering to reconnect with my roots that brought me here as a keynote speaker. I was supposed to inspire the youth. Show them there's a legal way out. Crazy thing is, she goes on vacation instead of being here to explain everything. Sabrina's convinced I lost something priceless here. I don't know what it could possibly be, but I'm glad I came," he said while staring into her eyes.

"I'm glad too, Bradley," Nicole replied in a sexy voice accompanied by a mischievous smile.

"Check please!"

*

Bradford fumbled around with the radio until Nicole placed her hand over his and found the quiet storm station they use to spend countless nights together listening to. She was unaware the problem was not finding a station, but the fact that he seldom drove made the dashboard controls a little foreign to him. They pulled in front of her apartment and parked just in time for the group Guy to sing "let's chill" on the radio. Bradford let back the sunroof and put all four windows down before turning the key to the auxiliary position.

"Brad, are you trying to seduce me? Don't you think you're moving a little bit fast? I'm a Lady. I can't just put out for the Olive Garden. Now, that island coast adventure might have got you lucky," she said in a playful manner.

He leaned over the middle leather armrest and found her welcoming lips and tongue meeting him eagerly. Everything was perfect, nothing could ruin this moment.

"Mom, What are y'all doing!" Mary screamed, startling both of them.

"Well, uh, it just sort of happened... Wait a minute. Why am I explaining something I can't explain to you anyway? I'm the mom, you're the child. Now, what are you doing out here, young lady?" Nicole asked out of frustration while fixing her dress and trying to keep an authoritative stance through her obvious embarrassment.

"You forgot to buy groceries so I couldn't make lunch for tomorrow. There's nothing to fix for breakfast in the morning," Mary answered, making sure to show her braces with every word used.

"Hop in, I'll run you both to the store," Bradford offered.

The ride to Wal-Mart or "Willy World" as they referred to it, was in total silence. Bradford continued to peek in the rearview mirror at Mary from time to time. It was important what she thought of him. The parking lot was packed with customers, causing him to circle the parking lot before dropping them off in front of the entrance, then finding a parking space. Nicole and Mary grabbed a shopping cart and disappeared behind the automatic sliding doors. Bradford caught up to them and picked up a small basket and decided to do a little shopping himself.

"Brad.....! Is that you? Well, I'll be damned, it is you." He was caught in the motion of teasing fruit for firmness when a woman grabbed him from behind and squeezed him. Bradford turned around to a hypnotizing pair of light brown eyes, close cut blonde hair, red lipstick and curves that left him at a loss for words.

"It's me, Cora. You should know who I am as much as we used to mess around when we was little," she said with a little devilish smile.

"Wow... it has been a long time. How have you been, what have you been up to?" he asked, trying not to stare at her bulging curves.

"I've been okay. I strip at a club called "Magic City" in Portsmouth, and "Minx" in the Beach. You should come see me next time you're in town. You won't be disappointed, I promise."

"I just might do that. You got a number? I'll make sure to have my personal assistant place that on my schedule. You remember Sabrina don't you?"

"Of course, she stays in touch with the hood, and show love to a bitch. Here's my card, give me a call, maybe we can grab a bite or something before you leave," Cora whispered before slowly walking away, making sure her ass swayed and jiggled with each step.

A song made by an old friend played instantly in his mind. "It gotta be jelly cause jam don't shake like that!"

"Are you enjoying yourself, Brad?" Nicole asked after catching him watching Cora for a few seconds. Bradford turned around to see her standing with a shopping cart full of groceries.

"No... Uh... What are you talking about?" he asked with a look of guilt clearly written on his face.

"Nothing.... Men... Can you go find Mary while I ring everything up? You can do that can't you?" she said with an attitude before walking away.

Bradford scanned a couple of aisles before finding Mary with a gallon of milk and a box of Little Debbie Zebra Cakes. "Come on, your mom's at the checkout counter."

Once at the counter, Bradford offered to pay for the groceries. Nicole gave him a look that could kill, and made sure he knew they didn't need his money by paying herself. Mary and Bradford were taking the groceries to the truck when Mary gave him a little woman's insight. "She caught you, didn't she? I thought guys got smarter the older they get. You never look at another woman while you're with a woman... and she put on her special panties for you."

What could he say to that? He tried to find a reasonable rebuttal but failed miserably.

The ride back was quiet and full of tension with Nicole's lips pouting and her arms crossed. Bradford helped take the groceries in the house. "Nicole, can I see you outside before I leave? Good night, Mary, and thanks for everything. Next time I'm in town, whatever you want to do is on me, young lady."

"Yeah Brad, what do you want?" Nicole spat as soon as they were just outside the hallway door.

He felt like a teenager again, going through one of their issues where she'd responded in the same way. "That kiss was kinda nice earlier. I was wondering if I can have a little more of where that came from?"

"No, you didn't just say that after I caught you staring at Cora's ass in the store not even fifteen minutes ago! You got a lot of nerve, buddy. Money can't have that much of an effect that you've completely become such an insensitive, arrogant bastard that you'd think I would kiss you after that little stunt you pulled. Why don't you go ask her about kisses and all of the above? The strip club is still open, just like her legs... you just nasty. I ain't forgot about y'all two."

"Okay, you're making a mountain out of a molehill. All I did was look. I have eyes and there's no way I could miss her. I'm not your man, remember? I'm assuming Larry's her father, who you started seeing behind my back," Bradford revealed aloud for the first time in over thirteen years.

"Behind your back, negro please, you ran off to college with your precious Sabrina and expected me to believe she just happened to attend school in the same city as you and didn't even tell me you were planning to go! OOhhh! If you only knew... I actually thought you had changed but oh no, you're still that same selfish son-of-a-bitch you've always been! You got one thing right. I'm not your woman, thank God! And for your information, I don't have time for male friends. Mary does have a father but it's not Larry. For your bee's wax, he only came around to comfort me after the heartbreak of you running off to college.

We became good friends and nothing became of it until many years later. I was waiting for you like a "pure-tee fool"... Even after all this time, if I am gonna be completely honest with myself, a part of me has still been waiting. Look what you've made me do. Messing up my makeup... please... just leave, Brad... Go... maybe seeing you wasn't such a good idea after all," she said softly before walking away with tears streaming down each cheek.

The situation had unraveled and spun out of control. Bradford had never really had control or answers. Now all he seemed to have was questions since he'd returned home. He decided he'd figure it out once inside the apartment until the sight of Mary stopped him in his tracks.

"What did you do to my mom?" Mary asked as tears began to form in her eyes.

"I don't know sweetheart... I truly and honestly have no idea what I did."

Denial

"Bust that thang open for a real nigga," pulsated throughout the club by Rich Gang. A few bottles of Cristal, Ace of Spades, Ciroc, and Patron sat on the table while Bradford continued to nurse his wounds and drown in each confusing thought. He knew taking Nicole's advice to go see Cora was not what she really meant. It was not only wrong, but distasteful, yet he couldn't resist the urge. Bradford had no doubt that if Nicole ever discovered what he was doing she would never forgive him. Though she had no right to feel that way, he cared about her thoughts and feelings.

"Smack my ass. This V.I.P. treatment baby, stick your finger in it like you did back in da day... It's alright now. I can handle it, daddy," Cora yelled as both thighs and ass cheeks bounced like an earthquake was in the building.

He tried his best to hold onto the many confused and uncertain thoughts about Nicole and why she became so upset out of nowhere, it seemed. Bradford reasoned that maybe he should have been more discreet when watching Cora's ass earlier but even now it was a major distraction. Cora was vying for his full attention just as she had purposely done so in the store. Bradford knew she was paid to keep dudes' attention focused on her body and the fantasy of seeing more, hoping to touch it. From the look of the white Mercedes she asked him to meet her by outside, after her shift, employee of the month was an understatement.

"Don't be shy. I know the sign says don't touch the dancers but that's for legal purposes. As long as she lets you, it's all good. Let me bust it open for you, shit!" she said before spreading her pussy lips so wide that pink was all Bradford could see. Cora slid down to her knees and unbuckled his belt with her teeth, exposing his dick, and swallowed him whole into her throat in one motion while looking up into Bradford's eyes with an expression of a cat that had just been caught with a mouse tail hanging out of its mouth.

Bradford's eyes rolled in the back of his head from the combination of seeing that look, and the indescribable pleasure he was currently experiencing.

CHAPTER TEN

Unorthodox

THE VIEW FROM THE TOP of her head moving up and down, coupled with the extreme pleasure her lips, and the inside of her mouth were providing to his dick were pushing him to the point of no return. "Damn girl, what are you trying to do to me? That's it, Cora, right there baby," Bradford quivered.

"Cora, do I look like Cora to you! I come here and allow myself to be completely vulnerable and this is how you treat me?" Sabrina said before running into the bathroom crying.

"I'm sorry; I'm so sorry Brina, I..." Bradford's body was as rigid as a piece of steel. He woke up to quiet, dread, shame, confusion, a hard-on, and a hangover. The strange surroundings were obviously a hotel located somewhere in the Hampton Roads area. One thing was certain, he had to leave the state, and fast. He stumbled into the bathroom and empty the contents of his stomach while the pounding in his head drowned out the awful sounds of constant heaving. Whatever priceless thing Sabrina claimed was in Tidewater had eluded him, as it had growing up. The first thing on his agenda was aspirin, solid food, and ginger ale to settle his stomach, then the quickest route out of his current nightmare.

"Knock knock, housekeeping. Mr.Williams, checkout time is in ten minutes. Are you staying with us another night?" a pleasantly feminine voice with a Spanish accent asked from the other side of the room's door.

"No, I will be downstairs to checkout momentarily. Thank you," he replied.

"And thank you, Mr. Williams, for your stay here at the Westin. Please come again." The voice said before knocking on another guest's room door further down the hall.

Bradford composed himself and stepped out of the bathroom to a glass of water extended in one hand, and the other hand of his blonde assistant holding two extra strength Tylenols. Her hair was pinned up,somehow seeming to hide the evidence of hair pins. The 6-foot driver, also present, was motionless, awaiting instructions.

After a quick shower and shave, Bradford was draped in Armani. His assistant brought him up to speed on how he wound up in the present room instead of the timeshare he owned. She also informed him that Nicole had called several times, as well as Cora who was referred to as, "the young woman that provided him with entertainment." Bradford had a gag clause placed in every contract that had to be signed in front of a licensed notary before employment was even considered. This served mostly as a legal umbrella because he dealt with high-end clients, groundbreaking discoveries, some practices that broke the law depending on who you asked, and the occasional immoral act.

"I'm going to go speak with the hotel's manager. I will be sure to reward him for his discretion, and last-minute accommodations," the assistant said before walking in the opposite direction of Bradford. The bodyguard excused himself to bring the car around to the private exit.

*

"What happened to the Range Rover?" Bradford quickly asked after seeing a gold sports car. The gold Maserati Quattroporte SQ4, four-door luxury sports sedan came with all the bells and whistles. Although Bradford leased most of his vehicles for convenience and business, this particular vehicle had his undivided attention. Bradford was impressed with how the eight speed transmission handled the five hundred and three horse powered engine. He enjoyed the ride so much he completely missed the scenery he looked forward to on the way back to the private airstrip.

"Good afternoon, Mr. Williams. I am Captain Armstrong. We will be taking off momentarily. Please enjoy your meal. The server has been instructed to grant your every wish," the captain said with a smile before shaking Bradford's hand and returning to the cockpit.

The bodyguard could be seen sitting in the Maserati as the plane began to lift off the ground.

"Is everything okay, Mr. Williams, is there anything I can do for you?" the server asked while purposely showing the cleavage of her full breasts, and licking her lips slow and seductively.

"Why yes, tell the pilot to turn around," Bradford said emotionless after ending the call that left a vague look across his face.

CHAPTER ELEVEN

"SO WHAT WAS HE LIKE? I mean, he seemed alright at the school but you got to chillax wit'em."

"Okay, what part about I don't want to talk about him did you not understand, and why did we have to come all the way to Greenbrier Mall? Lynhaven, Pembroke, Military Circle, and Macarthur are all featuring the same movie, besides,the Lego movie is not what I picked anyway." Mary pointed out to her annoying, nosey friends.

Why her mother had gotten so upset stirred something inside her that couldn't be explained yet. Mary asked what Bradford did but her mother claimed he did nothing wrong. That it was all her fault because she'd never been fully honest with him. Mary then harassed her grandmother until Gertrude revealed their young love was destroyed by her own constant meddling and doubt.

Gertrude explained that she wasn't Nicole's mother. In fact, Nicole's mother was Gertrude's daughter, and had been killed by a jealous boyfriend many years ago, leaving Nicole to raise. She went on to explain that Bradford never had a fair shake with her mother because in her mind every young man wanted to take Nicole from her, like Nicole's mother's boyfriend had. All of this was too much to process at once for a thirteen-year-old mind about to start junior high school.

"Y'all go ahead and save me a seat," Mary instructed after she caught a glimpse of a familiar face moving in the crowd. 'It can't be... This is all I need right now,' she thought to herself. After peeking through the window of every department store, and discreetly surveying each kiosk, she entered JCPenney department store and headed to the men's department.

"Yes, I would like to have each of these ties matched with a solid colored oxford shirt and dress slacks. Throw in a pair of black and brown belts, and shoes while you're at it. Here's my JCPenney card, have it sent along with my things to this address, thank you."

Mary quickly grabbed a few ties after seeing him exit the store. "Excuse me, that guy that was just here dropped these. He also overpaid me for running a few errands. My cellphone is dead and I need to call him before he gets too far away from the mall."

"I'm sorry but the customer you are referring to only left an address," the full figured white sales clerk replied.

"Oh, okay. Can you call me a cab and send it to that address?" Mary said as maturely as possible. She then walked around the store, browsing until the cab arrived. "HD 2 LEAVE BRB TTYL" Mary started texting and sent to her friends while the cab driver maneuvered onto the interstate. She had no idea where they were headed so she paid close attention to each exit, to make sure she would be able to retrace her steps. Before long they were exiting and cruising down Battlefield Blvd. The driver pulled in front of Chesapeake General Hospital to pick up another customer. "We're here, that will be ....fifteen dollars."

*

The main entrance was filled with an atmosphere of uncertainty, yet calm. Mary tried to understand why the address would be a hospital, unless... She suddenly knew which floor to look for on the massive directory board.

The nurses' station sat in between all of the rooms on both sides of the hall as she exited the elevator.

"Larry Smith's room please?" Mary asked while struggling to mask her anger.

"Larry, oh yes, we all know Larry here. He's all over the hospital. So I can see how you ended up on the wrong floor. This is the maternity floor.I doubt you will find him in his room because he rarely is. You can try though. Take the elevator two floors up to room 1205," the chipper, informative, skinny white nurse wearing a bob hairstyle rattled off effortlessly.

Mary took the elevator as instructed, all the while fighting back tears that seemed to escape one eyelid at a time regardless of how hard she fought. She now knew the truth; her father cheated on her mother, made a new life while abandoning them, and was now having a new baby. Mary pulled herself together as best she could before placing her hand on the large dull polished metal door latch to room 1205.

CHAPTER TWELVE

THE UNIFORM WHITE AND LIGHT colors throughout the room's decor became just as drab as a room draped in different hues of black. Constant shuffling of feet in and out of the room, or up and down the hallways had become a beautiful irritant that signaled to the brain he would see one more day, perhaps.

The reality of experimental treatments, change in medications, emergency surgeries, doctors, interns and specialists who were probably more interested in career advancement than saving his life, were not enough to discourage his will to live. Most mornings, the highlight of the day involved a sponge bath, watching some shapely nurse bend over, or pretending to be asleep while gossip or details of his condition were being discussed before recording them onto his medical chart clipboard. Waking up to muster a smile and exude positive energy had become harder each day. Something was unusual about this particular morning. He knew someone was in the room with him, but who? Whoever it was had not made a sound other than light breathing. It had been made crystal clear, by him, that he was to have no visitors, yet here someone was. Slivers of light and distorted images of color flooded both retinas as he barely opened each eyelid.

"I know you're awake. I can see your eyes moving around under your eyelids. Everyone here speaks so highly of you. If only they knew the real coward you are. Where is your family? You gave up everything for them. The least they can do is be here for whatever reason you are here. I don't see any cards, balloons, flowers…The gift shop is right by the entrance to the hospital!"

He instantly opened both eyes to the first syllables of the familiar voice. Next a roller coaster of emotions took control of his body as he heard the hurt in his visitor's voice and felt tears flow from his own eyes. He understood the anger and hurt, but all of what was said didn't make sense. "Calm down. There's obviously a lot that needs to be discussed. I'm afraid you haven't been told everything, and since you're here by yourself, your mother and grandmother must have no idea where you are…. Am I right?" Larry asked with apparent shame and sympathy.

The room, which thirty minutes prior symbolized hopelessness and a strong urge to surrender, had just become a lot brighter.

"You are truly the perfect mixture of your mother and father. I have thought about you every day since....." he stopped, afraid too much may be said.

"Since.... What? All lies! You're a liar! Since.... When? You can't even say it, can you? Since you left me and my mom and had another family," Mary replied out of deep hurt and resentment.

Larry allowed silence to absorb the tension he felt in the room. He calmly exhaled before slowly dragging his hands across both sides of his face. The main reason for his disappearance was the reasoning that his absence would be far less painful than watching him deteriorate daily before his loved ones' eyes. Now Larry was faced with exposing the other reason. Mary's hair had grown, along with her stature, but other than that, she was still the spitting image of her mother. "I don't know where you got the notion you can speak to me like you have but I'm going to excuse you, young lady, in light of the confusion and misinformation caused by my leaving. I didn't leave you and your mother for another family. There is no other family. I have been in this hospital diagnosed with cancer. Waiting…

"Oh my god. Daddy, I'm so sorry. You don't have to do this by yourself. I'm here now," Mary said before walking to his bedside and holding his hand.

"That's so sweet but I wouldn't want you to see me after the different treatments I have to go through. We can call each other everyday though. By the way, how did you find me, and where does your mother think you are?" Larry asked with a stern look of concern.

Mary's demeanor changed instantly with his tone and line of questioning. "Well… See… what had happened was… I'm supposed to be at the mall seeing a movie but I saw you and followed you from JCPenney," Mary said before flashing an innocent smile.

Larry's face went through several changes that would signal he was in pain to the untrained eye but it was actually projections of his indecisiveness. His present condition was enough to drop on her right now, so he questioned if opening his mouth or keeping it closed was most important in the grand scheme of things. So far, everyone involved used avoidance, ignorance, and deceit to satisfy their part played in the situation. Now that he was confronted with the aftermath of those decisions, something had broken loose inside of him.

"Baby, I need you to come lay with me. What I'm about to tell you is going to change everything. I just need you to know that everybody around you only wanted the best for you. Sometimes adults make the wrong decisions for the right reasons. Your mother, grandmother and I have tried our best to protect you since the day your mother found out she was pregnant. Just promise me you won't hate us for what I'm about to tell you. Please try to understand your best interest is what we were looking out for."

"Okay, Daddy, just tell me whatever it is," Mary said while lying on his chest and listening to the weak sound his heart made.

Larry signaled for her to come closer and began to whisper a confession that felt like he was pushing the little life left in him, from his body. Tears flowed freely as he tried to regulate his breathing. "See, I worked at an adoption agency when your mother and I started dating."

"No... Wow... Why? Mary climbed off the bed and tried to steady herself while each thought spun clockwise and counterclockwise simultaneously. She looked into Larry's face and saw the tears of a total stranger. The words he had just spoken were either the truth from a stranger, or a lie from her father. Before her brain had enough time to fully process the information, the machine in the room started beeping loudly and flashing.

"Code blue! Cold blue! Ma'am you're going to have to step outside the room while we attempt to resuscitate the patient!" a nurse shouted at Mary but she could not hear, speak, nor move. A movie of unspeakable horror was playing right before her very eyes... she was unable to turn her head... not even to blink.

CHAPTER THIRTEEN

LEI

THE ALL WHITE ON WHITE 2014 Bentley GT convertible purred with an aggressive low growl as the tires gripped each winding curve of the coastline, revealing a new breathtaking view with each turn. The backseat was filled with expensive designer merchandise waiting like a kite for just the right amount of wind gust to escape its owner. The driver met the valet at the entrance of the hotel without a word, whisked through the lobby, and found a beach cabana by the infinity pool.

"Would you like one, Mrs. Williams, and will you also be attending the hotel cabaret? A private room and complimentary champagne has been reserved for your convenience," a skimpy clad young female from the hotel staff offered.

She waved off the waitress and slowly nodded at the Adonis figure standing before her, glistening with water creeping down each fold of his sculpted physique. It quickly became apparent she had been enjoying the view a little too much when he kindly extended the tray he was holding filled with a variety of colorful tropical mixed drinks. She politely took one and seductively sipped from its rim to hide the embarrassing look and blushing that was now creeping onto her face.

"Please enjoy yourself, Mrs. Williams. You will find there are many activities, shopping and sightseeing on the island. The people here are very friendly, cultured and knowledgeable. The hotel provides a guide, or you can explore the island on your own," he said in the native accent before politely excusing himself.

It was obvious that the server's last comment was pertaining to her recent shopping spree. She slowly reclined and raised her left arm to look at her bare ring finger. "Mrs. Williams, I could truly get used to this."

*

The sun peeked between the thick expensive curtains and slowly warmed Sabrina's body beneath the sheets. She tossed and turned, determined to hold on to the most peaceful sleep she'd ever experienced, compliments of the 1,800 thread count Egyptian cotton bedding.

"Hello," she slurred out into the phone's receiver with her eyes still closed, hair wildly positioned all over her head, and clothes mixed with the suite's king-size comforter sprawled all over the floor.

"Aloha, Mrs. Williams, you have a ten o'clock at the Spa Grande. We offer the crystal energy massage to revitalize, and lemongrass butter application followed by a Japanese treatment of Reiki which soothes muscles and brings balance using intricate hand placement. This holistic process lasts for 80 minutes and works wonders for those guests who have enjoyed the island nightclubs the previous night. Everything is complimentary with your suite. I'm just calling to confirm your appointment," the caller on the other end explained.

Sabrina let most of the conversation prattle along before her brain decided to make sense of it instead of resting as she'd planned. Her head was still under the sheets and the receiver's cord was being stretched to its limits to reach the side of the bed. "Okay, okay, fine. I'll be down there in twenty minutes," she answered before leaving the receiver on the bed to prevent any further disruptions. Sabrina got up after surrendering to the reality of never being able to regain the level of restfulness the phone call had disturbed.

The massive bathroom was filled with marble, glass and gold fixtures. The shower was all glass and had a large shower head with two body pulses that promised a luxurious experience. The terry cloth towels seemed to do more than just dry her skin as she searched each surface area for wetness. After a lengthy hygiene routine, Sabrina returned to her room to find everything organized, including the bed being made. The dining room table had a fresh bouquet of flowers soaking in a crystal vase half filled with water, centered in the middle with several dishes of fruits, waffles, eggs, bacon and various juices.

*

"Excuse me," Sabrina apologized to anyone paying attention, after a small belch accompanied by much dreaded acid reflux. Unsure if the previous night's drinking, the large assortment of breakfast foods, or the Bloody Mary with a small stem of celery held in her left hand was the cause, or the solution. With cucumbers covering each eye, a thick slimy green substance coating her face, and a thick, white, hotel initials embroidered terry cloth robe covering her body, the experience continued to be just what she needed.

"Excellent choice, ma'am," the female nail technician said after Sabrina chose coral pink to have painted on her nails and feet. The aroma of scented candles, freshly picked flowers, sweet scented massage oils, along with soft music playing at almost an inaudible volume provoked yawning, and caused water to slip from between her eyes. Sabrina dozed off and woke up to her own snoring, a few slight giggles from the hotel staff, and light shaking used to let her know the treatment was finished. She pulled herself together, said her goodbyes, and headed towards the elevators.

The large elevator was designed with see through one-way mirrors reserved for privileged stays. A well dressed concierge politely asked, "Which floor, Mrs. Williams?" before pressing the number she gave, and then returning to an almost lifeless position at the rear of the elevator. The awkward silence was finally broken by a slight jolt almost unnoticed when the elevator reached the designated floor.

Sabrina quickly made her way towards the lavish suite while mentally choosing from the variety of activities she would try and later boast about experiencing on this particular trip. The phone could be heard ringing before she reached the large mahogany French doors. Sabrina quickly opened them and made her way to the phone. "Aloha... yes, put it through. Hello.... Yes, this is she. Is everything alright?" Sabrina vaguely remembered asking before the reply caused her to drop the phone in disbelief. After several hours of crying she pulled herself together.

"I need to be on the next available flight to Norfolk, Virginia. Private, commercial, doesn't matter, money is no object. If it's commercial, make it first class, business is as low as I'll accept. I understand this is short notice, there's an extra thousand in it for you if you can have me off the ground within the hour," Sabrina promised before hanging up and frantically throwing her clothes in each suitcase.

CHAPTER FOURTEEN

2014

COLORS, SOUNDS, NUMBNESS, AND DRYNESS of mouth refused to be acknowledged by her proper senses. Several people's lips moved but understanding only came from their facial or body positioning and motions. 'Get it together girl, you can do this. Just fix your makeup, pull your hair back, and smile.' Only happy thoughts replayed in her mind as if he were present repeating those very words to her again. The tears began to flow once again. The huge dark designer shades sitting on her face concealed both swollen eyes well. Foundation, blush, eyeliner, and mascara could only withstand so much abuse before they simultaneously threw in the towel, regardless of the big name labels used on their price tag. She allowed herself to fall in step with the assembly line of bodies moving towards the double doors.

The inside was breathtaking. Thick maroon plush carpeting spread out as far as the eyes could see. The seating was made of thick, rich, mahogany wood and a matching maroon cushioning. Huge stained glass windows limited the sunlight intrusion throughout the building.

"So good to see you, I just wish it was under better circumstances. I would ask Larry to invite you to family dinners and such…You know you were supposed to be my daughter-in-law? He looks so peaceful…don't he… I'm just glad my baby is in a better place."

Sabrina heard the words being spoken to her as well as feeling the light patting of a comforting hand, but the only response her body would yield was a constant stream of tears. She promised herself to keep her emotions under control, and fought so hard up until this very point to hold on to that promise. Larry had been her first official boyfriend. She could only stare in a daze at the fragile ghost of his image prepared by the funeral home. Sabrina was shocked to find out he kept his battle with cancer a secret from everyone and chose to reveal it through the use of a funeral service that had done such a horrible job.

"Mildred, you raised a fine example of a man. He extended each and every one of those invitations. I just thought it best to keep things between us as less complicated, and awkward as possible. There were still unresolved issues between the two of us, and I thought there was plenty of time left to address them," she explained to his mother before giving her a heartfelt, comforting hug.

Mildred began to sob uncontrollably before both legs gave out and Sabrina was forced to help walk her to the limo headed to the family burial plot.

Mildred Wilson had lost a mother to breast cancer, a father to prostate cancer, now her only son. The numbness she felt inside was not only familiar but welcomed. She looked at the reflection of the stranger staring back at her. At sixty years old, Mildred stood five feet even with smooth sensitive skin, soft eyes, plum dyed hair and a welcoming presence. Her mannerisms and particular style of dress was always conservative, refusing to become one of those people unable to come to terms with the reality of "getting up" in age. She adopted a few styles of the younger crowd such as plum dyed hair but prided herself in making of special choices that set her apart from the women her age trying to hang with their daughters frequenting clubs with younger crowds, and wearing clothes made of revealing material, cut too low or too high.

The bags drooping under the empty eyes of the old hag that slightly resembled her were horrible. After looking from left to right and realizing this woman would continue to mimic her, denial allowed her mind to drift off to intimate memories of special moments shared with her baby boy.

"Ms. Wilson... Ms. Wilson, we're here... Ms. Wilson." The chauffeur spoke softly. Mildred continued to stare aimlessly at the peaceful scenery of emerald green grass surrounding headstones made up of grays and neutral colors. The soft feeling of light, yet increasing pressure of someone's hand squeezing hers caused Mildred to turn and lock eyes with a beautiful face streaming with tears that she'd missed more than she ever cared to admit.

"I know it's hard but I'm here. We're all here. Each step is supposed to be easier. I don't know how true that is but I know the first step means getting out of the car. Every step after that is in God's hands. Your son would want to see that pretty smile and strength you've always shown," Sabrina whispered softly while rocking Mildred in her arms before patting her hand and wiping both of their tears.

"Hello Mary. I know this isn't easy for you. Your dad was a good man. I promised the next time I was in town we could do whatever you like. Well, seems like I'll be here a couple of weeks longer than I expected to; so just have your mother call me," Bradford said with sadness and sympathy.

"Why are you even here? You've never liked my dad. You made my mother cry. You never come around and probably only came around to check on the money my mom gets which ain't for no essay so you can keep your money and stay out of our lives!" Mary ranted as tears flowed uncontrollably before she stormed off, disappearing amongst the crowd of mourners now leaving the burial site.

"Mary! Come back here, young lady and apologize to Brad this instant!" Nicole said, attempting to go after her before Brad firmly grabbed her arm.

"Let her go, it's okay. She's obviously taking Larry's death hard. We should all be allowed to grieve in our own way," Bradford explained although the pain shown on his face was more the result of Mary's words than the actual funeral.

"That may be so but it doesn't give her the right to be disrespectful. I'm so sorry. I just put her on punishment for leaving her friend, and having them lie to their mothers for her while she went off who knows where, doing who knows what. Then I get this call... I didn't mean for all of that to come out," Nicole recanted after she realized how easily she became comfortable sharing her thoughts with him.

"I understand. Single parenting is not easy from what I'm told. Mary's a teenager with a good head on her shoulders. Everything will be fine, you'll see."

"I'm glad someone can see that far ahead because insight is a gift I don't have at the moment," Nicole confessed before climbing inside her car and closing the door, starting it, and letting the window down.

"I know you were trying to reach me and I never returned your calls... I..."

"This is not the time. Don't mean to cut you off but I see Mary heading in this direction and I need to deal with her. I'll call you later and we'll talk," Nicole quickly said, more focused on her daughter's state of mind than talking to Brad.

"Okay, just remember, take it easy on her," Bradford advised before walking away.

*

Bradford loosened his black tie before unbuttoning the top button of his black Armani dress shirt. He carefully took off the black Armani suit jacket and laid it across the empty bar stool next to him. "Bartender, Hennessey on the rocks... No, make that a double."

Kelly's tavern was basically a bar and grill chain that held a relaxed yet conservative crowd atmosphere.

"Excuse me, sexy, anyone sitting here, or did you have your jacket here to reserve this seat for me?" A sultry female voice whispered in his ear.

Bradford played it cool by not turning around, yet showing all of his pearly white teeth with the smile that she provoked. "No one is sitting there; perhaps I've been waiting on you all of my life. Why don't you just make yourself as comfortable as possible on that stool and order whatever you like."

"I see. I'll have a dirty martini and an extra tall glass of you," she replied while stroking his newly smooth shaven bald head.

"Whoa, that's enough. That move got me so hard I couldn't leave right now even if I wanted to."

"Mmmm.... Promise?" she asked in a seductive tone while slowly removing her index finger from her mouth, exposing a newly manicured coral pink fingernail.

"Okay, that's enough, Brina. Let's stop before it gets out of hand," Bradford said with unconvincing seriousness.

"If you say so... I wanted to see how far we'd push the envelope before one of us tapped out... Bradford you're no fun," Sabrina whined in a seductively playful voice.

"How's his mom holding up? I saw you riding in the family limo. I had your replacement track you down and make sure you knew Larry died although you were on vacation because I knew you'd never forgive me if I hadn't," Bradford revealed before swallowing another swig.

"Mildred is a tough old bird. You know her, that young spirit and plum colored hair will be vibrant again in no time. She took an Ambien and was sleeping peacefully like an angel when I left. As far as ruining my vacation, you better had,took some time to find me and relay the message.... And there's no replacing me by the way," she said before playfully punching him in the arm.

"Seriously, all jokes aside.... Brina, how are you holding up?"

CHAPTER FIFTEEN

"HELLO CHILD, AIN'T YOU A sight for sore eyes? Haven't seen you in a while. Turn round, let me get a good look at cha... My, how you've grown. You're becoming such a beautiful young lady, look just like your momma when she was your age," Gertrude said before giving Mary a warm embrace, as the reality that her only great grandbaby had grown up, and was growing further apart from her each day. She also noticed the change from happy and sweet, to angry at the mention of uncanny resemblance between mother and daughter.

"Hey Grandma. I mean, Gerttie. It hasn't been that long. Anyway, I've missed you. How have you been?"Mary asked more out of a need to distance herself from a conversation she knew her mother Nicole would chime in on since she was also present. Mary left the multipurpose room area of Seatack recreation center before her grandmother could reply, heading towards the swimming pool.

Nicole entered the room just as her daughter exited, which she knew wasn't a coincidence. "Hello, mother. I see Miss Thing came in here calling herself mad with me, let me tell you. That granddaughter of yours snuck off with some boy and had her little friends lying for her. I'm taking the little heifer to see if she's having sex so I can put her little hot ass on birth control," Nicole said in an uneven tone with both hands balled into fist on her hips.

Gertrude exploded with laughter. What started as light amusement and a few smiles had bellowed into uncontrollable laughter. "I'm sorry, baby, but that's you all over again. Don't be so hard on the girl. You know all about puppy love, it's when they find what they think is real love, that's the problem. That girl ain't having sex. Her legs just as close, straighter than jailhouse cell bars. If it is a boy, and that's a big if, make her feel comfortable enough not to sneak around with him, invite him to dinner. Are you even sure it's a boy? Sex is the only reason for her to be sneaking around if a boy's involved. I think it's something else, mark my words. It'll all come out in the wash... she's still a virgin. I know my grandbaby," Gertrude said with confidence.

"Well, your grandbaby lied no matter where she was, or what she was doing. She never denied it was a boy, and she's been giving me a lot of attitude lately. She smelling herself."

Comeuppance

After an eight hour shift that involved everything from convincing a few senior citizens to try the new pudding manufacturer's donations, a last-minute bank deposit, misplaced rec. cards, several employees not showing up on time, and brown cupcake stains on a brand new white dress after two kids horse playing resulted in the pastry/fabric collision, Nicole was relieved to see her brand new silver 2014 Nissan Altima parked in front, anticipating her return.

"Hey, baby girl. I can always count on you to cheer me up, just thirty- five more payments and you're all mine," she said before lightly patting the center console armrest then starting the car's engine. Nicole allowed Mary to go home with Gertrude so they both could get a much needed break from one another. Placing Mary on punishment seemed to have more effect on mother than daughter. Mary had chosen the silent treatment as a response.

"She's a good girl, good grades, so what if there is a boy? I'll let her off punishment 'for it kills me," Nicole said to herself before giggling at the fact she'd been outwitted by a possible hormone raging teenager. The drive home was peaceful until it hit her. "Oh, oh shit... Oh no!" Nicole whined as a stream of urine escaped down both legs as she hustled out of the car, made it in the hallway, only to fumble with the keys in the deadbolt lock to her apartment. She transferred weight on each leg in a hopping motion that looked like hot coals were burning the bottom of her feet on the beautifully woven welcome mat.

The door opened with such force she almost fell on her face, leaving the front door centimeters from being closed as she hobbled towards the bathroom. The chocolate stained white dress now had blotches of urine to add to the party, and refused to be unzipped so she pulled it over her head. She plopped down on the commode and just let go. "Oh my God... That feels so good!" Nicole exhaled with both feet stretched as far apart as possible, turned inward while both knees touched, elbows rested on each knee, and her entire body went limp leaning inches above the wet lace panties stretched between her ankles. After washing the panties and each area of her white dress in the sink, both articles of clothing were hung on the shower rod to dry. Nicole backtracked, shut and locked her car and the front door, then made dinner before hearing the phone and catching it on the fifth ring. "Hey Mom, I was just about to call you and ask you to tell Mary I said, has she totally forgotten it's a school night? It's too late for her to be walking home so I'm on my way."

Aftermath

Nicole called in from work. Called Seatack Elementary School and briefed them on the situation before calling all of Mary's friends' parents, then her mother every hour on the hour. It had been at least 12 hours since the time her daughter left her mother's house, and 12 hours before an official missing persons report could be filed with the police precinct.

In hindsight, the gigantic issue they were having had quickly become a minuscule thought. Both her eyes were puffy and swollen from crying and she continued to focus on positive outcomes of the situation and fought the fatigue that became more and more aggressive by the minute. Nicole knew the absence of Mary's father, and then sudden death was the reasoning behind her acting out. She now had to face the possibility that therapy might be a needed course of action. Nicole walked towards her daughter's room and stood in the doorway enchanted by fond memories of Mary's first words, first day of kindergarten, first steps, tooth etc... It was painfully obvious that her mind used these memories as a defense mechanism to discourage the dreadful thing she was about to do.

*

Mary's bedroom was off limits. Nicole had agreed to these privacy terms from a growing young woman who had proven herself in every area trustworthy, in order to receive unlimited privacy. It had been over a year since Nicole last saw the room. The door was always shut, and since Mary washed her own laundry and had her own linen closet in her room, Nicole knew very little about her personal living quarters. There was obviously a bed, TV, and phone which every bedroom should have, Mary had explained years prior.

"Wow,"was all Nicole could muster while taking in everything before her.

The walls were painted royal blue with a white border of waves touching the ceiling. The light switch on the immediate right was a yellow SpongeBob cartoon character faceplate with the actual switch being the nose. The walls were filled with everything from coral reef seaweed, starfish, whales, jellyfish and every other imaginable sea creature. The bedspread, pillowcases, curtains, and stuffed animals were all aligned around Sponge Bob, or some other character from the cartoon.

An overpowering wave of emotions swept over Nicole with each step across the threshold of Mary's room. She recalled the news fiasco of young children never found over the years. She would have a brief period of sympathy, add the families to her prayers for a few days, then have that tragedy replaced with some other more current calamity.

The thought of her life being dissected by police and scrutinized by neighbors and friends, not to mention her own guilt was almost unbearable. Nicole avoided alerting her church, Grace True Vine Pentecostal, though they meant well. Church gossip and holier-than-thou attitudes might force her to do or say something not only ungodly but downright devilish. She didn't want the police presence seen in the neighborhood nor did she want them snooping through her daughter's personal belongings. So she'd have to do it herself. "Where do I begin?" she asked herself rhetorically before sitting at the foot of her daughter's bed and scanning the surroundings.

*

"Nothing!" Nicole screamed in frustration to herself as she threw a few recent pictures and a school yearbook in the middle of the SpongeBob bedspread. The search of the room's every inch turned up nothing. Nicole decided to read a few Bible verses before praying and putting everything back the way she found it.

"Well, I'll be damned," Nicole said in a calm surprised tone. A small black diary was right on the nightstand next to the bed under the large royal blue Bible that covered it. "October, blah, blah, blah use my mother's perfume. January use new fragrance. I knew my shit was getting low that little.... met Mike Mike. He understands what I'm going through. Went to see him." Nicole read excerpts from the diary aloud, trying to make sense of any clues hidden among the words in pages overlooked by reading in silence. The more she read the more she realized the mystery boy Mary had a secret crush on was named Mike Mike. She grabbed the yearbook, diary, and recent photos before leaving the room with a strong sense of hope. "Ma, I'm on my way, it's almost been twenty-four hours," she said into the phone receiver before hanging up and rushing out the front door.

*

A dining room light cut on, then off, before the living room light repeated the same ritual. Instead of getting the results intended by honking the horn, a voice appeared. "Hold your horses, I'm coming! You know I don't know where I place my purse. I just had it." Ten minutes later, midnight blue orthopedic shoes with nude knee high stockings could be seen stepping out of the closed-in porch's shadow and into the moonlight.

Gertrude wore a midnight blue skirt, pearl white blouse with ruffles that ran down the front, and a large green purse that signaled she was unable to find the one she'd been searching for. "I haven't stopped crying since you told me my grandbaby was not at home. I tell you... I know I have a habit of taking her side, but this time I'm going to give her a good scolding when we find her. Sister Shaw, Deacon Hastings, Pastor Palmer, Minister Drewit, my whole prayer group and bible study group all send their love," Gertrude announced before using a big toothed comb to massage her scalp in between the silver and gray finger wave hairstyle.

"Did you have to involve all of them? I was trying to keep this all as quiet as possible."

*

"Virginia Beach Police Department, how may I help you? Please hold while I transfer you to robbery-homicide," the small stickler was reciting into the receiver while holding up a finger to signal not to interrupt her. Her long brunette hair was pinned back from her face accenting her strong cheekbones. Both beady eyes, long narrow nose, and tight fitted uniform that hugged her athletic build were in line with her no-nonsense aurora. "Now, how may I help you both?"

Nicole watched as the woman at the information desk held the phone receiver to one ear, scanned through paperwork of some sort, and expected them to know who she was referring to.

"Yes... My daughter is missing."

"There's nothing we can do until she's been missing 24 hours," the information desk officer spat with no consideration.

"If you hadn't cut me off I would have explained that it has been 24 hours!"

"Are you certain ma'am?" she asked in a condescending tone.

Nicole took a deep breath before responding, "Yes, I am."

"Fill this out and have a seat."

Gertrude sat patiently in an uncomfortable chair, rocking with her out of place pocketbook laying across her lap. She watched in silence as Nicole scribbled answers to line after line of audacious questioning. Gertrude slowly patted Nicole's knee causing tears of frustration to be released from Nicole's eyes as she continued filling out each form.

"I'll take this back up to the window. You can go get some fresh air and fix yourself up. Let Mama handle that situation over there," Gertrude said with a mischievous smile.

Nicole knew her mother wasn't above causing a scene, no matter how religious she was. She also knew Gertrude could get away with it because of her age. A devilish grin spread across her face before she headed out of the front door and dialed a last resort phone number. "Hello, I don't mean to bother you but have you seen Mary? Well, she's missing and I've called everyone looking for her. I didn't want to involve you in my drama but I know the police might try to contact you for questions, so I wanted to give you a heads up. I'm at the precinct. That won't be necessary. Okay, second precinct on the boulevard."

CHAPTER SIXTEEN

Epiphany
2014

THE INTRUSION OF AUTOMOBILES, AIRPLANES, sunlight, and some mysterious body moving next to him disrupted his sleep. A pounding headache began to drum on cue, meaning further sleep was no longer an option. Soft strokes from the fingers attached to the unknown figure against his scrotum relieved winding tension. Bradford laid still and slowly began to focus on the technique he would use to get rid of his current company. He reached down to remove his BlackBerry from the crumpled pile of clothes lying on the floor. The cold draft that invaded the warmth sustained by their shared space, and the sheets, made him aware of their nakedness. "Brina, I don't know where I am but I'm with some strange woman. So come with a story and get rid of her. Fill me in on today's itinerary when you get here." Bradford quickly texted, pressed send, and waited on a response.

The woman next to him moved a few times before getting up and rushing to the bathroom. He could hear her pee, flush, then wash her hands.

"Thank God she washed her hands. At least I know she's clean," Bradford thought to himself. "Now who is she and how did she get in my bed?" he wondered.

"Don't know where I am, with some strange woman. The nerve of this nigga. How about you being a fucking man and be responsible for your own shit instead of having me lie for you!" Sabrina ranted after using the bathroom. "I don't mean to be rude but my head is hurting and my boss just sent a text which means I've got to go," she explained while sitting on the edge of the bed sliding on her panties. Sabrina stood up and hooked her bra around the front before spinning it around and staring into Bradford's eyes with her mouth wide open.

"Good morning to you too, Brina. I guess the first thing on the agenda is tell me how you really feel, being as that it's tell your boss off day," Bradford said sarcastically.

Sabrina stood embarrassed and at a loss for words. "Did we go there? I mean... Do you remember anything from last night that will explain how we got here?"

Bradford swung both feet over the edge of the bed and walked butt naked to the bathroom like a runway model. He took his time showering and shaving before returning to the bedroom to find Sabrina fully dressed. "Have you been able to locate anything of interest, commercial or residential, where the owner is willing to waive or cover all closing costs?"

"Brad, you were never supposed to hear what I said. It shouldn't have been said at all. So much has happened since I got back from vacation. The funeral... And... I'm still trying to get back in the groove of things," Sabrina explained. "We need to talk about this, about us."

"Did you find any potentials or not, Sabrina?" Bradford said straight to the point. She knew he was upset from his use of her full name, the tone he used was elusive.

"Yes, Mr. Williams," she answered in a submissive manner.

"Good. Coffee, black, no sugar. I have a feeling this is going to be a long day. By the way, while you were gone I had the pleasure of running into a few people from the neighborhood. Seems as though you've been able to keep in contact with quite a few of them. What I wanted to ask you is, what is the logical explanation for me paying money every month to Nicole for her daughter's college education when there is at least five years until she graduates high school? Did you know Nicole was pregnant before she got with Larry? Which means she was messing with somebody she doesn't want me to know about, but you know all about that, don't you? What did I lose here that was so priceless? I hope it wasn't her?"

Sabrina flashed a half nervous smile before easing down on top of the nearest chair. She began fidgeting, tapping each finger on her legs in a piano playing motion, then rubbing both palms up and down her thighs.

"Well, we're always looking for a way to beat the IRS right? When I saw Nicole's daughter I came up with an answer. I set up a nonprofit organization to help disadvantaged kids go to college. She is the one who gave me the idea after reading a written contest she won that I sponsored. Nicole deposits money in a 529 college fund account each month. It's all tax deductible. Now, what you lost that is priceless is Mary's smile, optimism, and sense of family. I thought if you met her, maybe you would reconnect with the Bradford I met many years ago that cared more about community, helping people and family than money, and tax cuts," Sabrina explained astutely.

Bradford sat motionless as each word slowly sank in and went through a slow absorption. "Okay, I will admit I went through a series of memories, thoughts, emotions and feelings on this trip. This little stunt you pulled made me realize just how far I've come, and how many people I am now in the position to help. There are several famous people who came from the seven cities and forgot about the people who really need their help. I no longer want to be one of them. I've got an idea, but first what's the name of my non-profit?"

"Seatack. This area was built on the backs of our ancestors. I figured the area was called that before all the development we see today, so why not?"

"That's fine, I like the name. I assume you have a logo, business cards, promotions, public relations, and census people on standby? I'm thinking, place my properties on Section 8 listings and a few other programs that help qualified people get housing, transportation, as well as employment and education. Not a problem… just let me know your thoughts and I'll convey them to the right people. I'll get a couple of my associates involved, maybe host a Charity Dinner as well. I'm thinking since Mary is already a beneficiary of the program, why not make her mother one as well."

"I think she would be a great asset in furthering our vision, a spokesperson maybe?" Bradford said with excitement.

"I think that is an excellent idea. Would you like me to place a call to Miss Smith, or would you rather handle that on your own?"

"I've got it. She was supposed to call me about something anyway, and I was trying to give her some space. Now I have a valid reason for bothering her," Bradford said with a sneaky look and smile. "Speak of the devil. She's calling me right now. Hey, I was just about to call… No bother at all. No I haven't seen…. Police… Where are you now? I'll meet you there. Nonsense, I'm on my way," Bradford concluded with a weird feeling in the pit of his stomach.

"Is everything alright? You don't look so good," Sabrina asked.

"Mary's missing. I'll fill you in on what I know on the way to the 2nd police precinct. I assume you know where that is?"

Nicole fell into Bradford's arms as if there was no longer any use for muscle control of her legs. Her body released all tension and fear as gut-wrenching sobs escaped from the core of her being. It was now obvious to anyone who knew her that Bradford was not only a comfort zone but they both meant much more to each other than they were letting on.

"It's going to be okay, calm down, we're going to find her," Bradford assured while slowly walking her to a seat and wiping tears from her face. He took both of her hands into his. "I'm going to call in a few favors with WVEC, WAVY T.V. TEN and FOX NEWS, if I have your permission?"

Nicole simply nodded and hugged him with her head resting on his shoulder until she fell sound asleep.

"How are you Gerttie… how are you holding up?" Bradford asked with compassion in his voice.

"You know I lost her mother, I'm just trying to pray and stay positive. I'm afraid my old heart can't take another." Gertrude's eyes watered and her voice began cracking.

Bradford gently patted the back of her left hand with his right while making eye contact with Sabrina who also needed comforting. "Mary's fine, we're going to find her, don't you worry."

*

"Damn!! This vending machine should be fingerprinted and booked," Bradford said out of frustration.

"Are you okay? You know you don't have to be strong for everyone all the time. You're going to have to let someone take care of you at some point," Sabrina said before slowly sliding her fingers between his, and eventually holding hands with him.

Flashback 2001

Still exhausted from the night before, Bradford felt light-headed as he held on to her pelvis for dear life. He watched as sweat trickled down her neck, between each breast, or swan dived off her nipples onto his face as she rode him like an experienced horse jockey. The constant friction in awkward angles began to cause soreness that Bradford convinced himself was worth enduring. He found his mind reviewing the person known before this moment, and the person he was now watching bounce up and down while bending him in ways a manufacturer would have surely issued a warning against when using their product.

"Pull my hair. That's it. Spank me! Let's try something different. Yeah that's it. How's that feel?" she asked after getting on her hands and knees, then slipping him into her ass.

This new experience made both of his eyes roll in the back of his head. Bradford thrusted deeper and deeper into what felt like an endless abyss of pleasure. He almost fell off the bed trying to steady himself against her powerful return thrust.

A few weeks later........

"Hey Brad. I've been trying to call you for the last week. So,you going to play me like some chick you just met? You have been chasing me for years. I gave Monica the number because I thought we're both in a strange city and let's see where this takes us. We're both adults, you didn't have to put the duck game on me, and I sure as hell shouldn't have had to call from another number."

"You're right... And I'm sorry. It's just a lot. I mean... I don't want to mess up our friendship. I chased you so long when we were little that I had given up. The other night was more about me finally. I just... I wasn't prepared for all of that, any of that to tell you the truth," Bradford said before falling silent.

"I know it was a little extra, maybe too much for our first time. You don't have to say it. I just wanted it to be worth everything you went through over the years. Nobody knows so we can just forget it even happened. So… We cool?" Sabrina asked, not really meaning it but deciding after sleeping with Bradford and not getting the reaction she expected, there was no other choice.

"We cool Brina, cool."

"So, are you coming to homecoming or what?"

Flashforward to Present

They both stood staring at the rows of spiral racks filled with assortments of chips, nuts, and candy. Although a small bag of chips still hung off one rack, Bradford was able to look past it and calm down. He was used to solving any problem with money and resources, but today reality had continued relentlessly crashing through the huge bubble he spent so many years constructing. He kept a brave face and offered words of encouragement as if everything was impersonal but the truth was sharper than any surgical utensils.

"I'm going home in case she shows up there," Nicole said, interrupting their moment and noticing the change in the atmosphere when suddenly their hands quickly unlocked.

CHAPTER SEVENTEEN

THE VIRGINIA BEACH MUNICIPAL CENTER were large well kept buildings that resembled an office park filled with leased and vacant office suites, except for an abundance of police cars and vehicles with Virginia Beach city logos on the side of each front door. This area was composed of a jail, police precinct, city hall, and probation offices. Signs placed curbside allowed drivers to read the operation of the particular section of the building it stood before. Ample parking space was provided although a short walk might be necessary if your business was court related and before the hours of twelve to one o'clock. The grass, mulch, sidewalk, and parking lot were well maintained. The occasional high profile case drew a variety of news vans and reporters, as well as a celebrity or two showing up to address the court for some reason or another. Basically, this area was visited to pay speeding tickets or fines, appear in criminal, juvenile and domestic, or civil court, visit or bond someone out of jail, apply for a business license, pay taxes, or a probation appointment.

Overwhelmed

"Michael Perry, here to see whoever I'm assigned to. I was given this and told I had seventy-two hours to report here," he explained to a young high spirited receptionist talking on the phone, before passing release papers through the open sliding glass doors given to him by the corrections officer before he left prison.

The receptionist skimmed over each page before putting her current call on hold and placing another call. "Please have a seat, Mr. Perry, someone will be with you shortly," she said in between the conversation she was having.

He scanned the room and sorted out the ones on probation from the ones merely accompanying them. Somehow criminals had an air about them that could always be detected by him. The room had two vending machines, one for beverages, the other filled with snacks that included chips, nuts, candy bars, and breath mints. He found a seat in the best isolated position of the room and quickly rifled through the magazine selection catering to white families, or white stay-at-home housewives. "Better Homes and Gardens, REDBOOK, READER'S Digest or Time...Time it is," he said.

"Michael Perry, is there a Michael Perry present? Are you Mr. Perry? Please follow me then," said a woman peeking from behind the side door holding a thick manila file folder.

The actual office required a series of turns once you entered the hallway behind the secured door separating the waiting area from each probation officer. Diplomas, certificates, licensing, and a dollar bill covered in signatures were all framed and hanging on the walls.

"I'm Miss Stewart, Mr. Perry. I see you have been away from society for quite a while. Welcome back. I'm going to help you reintegrate, starting with transportation, obtaining a job, and emergency food stamps if you wish to apply. I require a urine screen every visit which will be once a week. This test will reveal any illegal drugs in your system so if you have substance abuse issues now is the time to let me know so I can get you some help. You are not allowed around firearms, other felons, housing areas flagged as red zones, or to leave the state without my permission. You cannot change your job or residence without alerting me. Any arrest or tickets must be reported immediately. I will make random home visits to see how you are adjusting, as well as stopping by your job. Make sure your employer is aware of this. So… Any questions?

*

The Union Mission was an all-male shelter that provided a refuge for those down on their luck. The ordinary building could easily be overlooked because it held no distinguishing characteristics. A line of society's outcasts could be seen carrying various sizes of plastic bags filled with clothes and hygiene products to meet the set curfew, or men sitting around outside in the morning were the only evidence of its existence from the side street it sat on between Granby Street, and Monticello Drive in Norfolk, Virginia.

Mike had used his mother's address to be released to, but found it hard to live there, knowing she died waiting for him to be released. Guilt and memories forced him to tolerate the awful scents, and ridiculous rules imposed at the shelter. The maneuver took great time and required him to stay at his mother's house long enough to catch his probation officers visit, but not too long that the shelter's curfew would be missed. After countless applications he was hired as a cashier at Exxon on the corner of Virginia Beach Boulevard, and Birdneck Road in Virginia Beach. This new employment would force him to live in the house he'd grown up in because the bus schedule did not run early enough to leave Norfolk and reach Virginia Beach for his shift.

"Pump five; please hang the nozzle up so I can reset it for you. Pump eight, your card has been declined. You have to come inside and pay cash, apply for a gas card, or call your bank to sort out the problem," Mike explained in an even tone.

At fifty-four he didn't look a day over thirty-five, especially since he decided to dye the white and gray infiltrating both his head and facial hairs. He stood six feet with jet black smooth skin, slanted eyes, and a small nose that gave him an Asian look. Mike was in perfect shape and conditioned. The gray uniform and black Air Force 1 sneakers were acceptable. It was the name tag that took getting used to. To hear total strangers randomly calling his government given name would take some getting used to when M. Perry, Mike Mike, or Mr. Perry was all he'd answered to for the last thirty-seven years.

"Yo, you, let me get a few Magnums, two blunts, a pack of Newports and thirty on the white Benz at pump eight since my card declined, smart ass, oops, or is it Mike?"

His temper flared before he could take his eyes off the candy rack he was taking inventory of. Her perfectly shaped ass stretched the short all white mini skirt she wore, exposing the bottom of each ass cheek, and the crotch of a see-through black lace thong. The light brown legs connected to this picture between the candy and snack aisle had black straps running along each one, stopping at six-inch white stilettos.

"I don't give a fuck about that bullshit, the customer's always right, or this job. You better watch how you talk to me," Mike said while approaching her with wild etched all over his face.

"Word.... okay, okay. Just let me get that and I'm on my way. I ain't got time for all the drama," she said after facing him with a bowleg stance, flashing a devilish smile, then scrolling past him towards the checkout counter.

Mike noticed she hadn't pulled down her skirt which was now showing a full frontal view of the laced thong and 3 inch gap between her legs. She saw him staring and wasn't bothered, nor did she make any attempt to block his view.

"Enjoying the view? This good pussy, she won't bite... Unless, you want her to; so when you get off?" she asked boldly.

Mike calmly unlocked the door, giving him access to the cash register area.

Everything about this woman was intimidating, from her physical appearance and attitude, to the expensive car and clothes. Her blonde close cut hair and sensual curves made him lose concentration, causing him to ring her purchase up twice.

"That'll be forty seven dollars and and eighty cents," he said while trying not to look into her piercing eyes.

"That's all you have to say? Don't tell me you one of dem down low brothers? Never took you for a back door bandit," she said before pushing a fifty dollar bill through the slot.

"Two dollars and twenty cents is your change. Here's your receipt, and would you like a bag?" Mike asked, hoping to hurry up and get rid of her.

"Use the change to buy some courage, scary lion," she spat out of anger before throwing the door open and crossing the parking lot. She made a sudden stop, lifted her skirt, and pulled her thong down to her ankles so he could get a good look. "Kiss my ass motherfucker!"

"You left your keys in here on the counter," Mike's voice announced over the intercom at pump number eight.

The walk back to get her keys redefined the phrase "Walk of Shame." She was unable to rationalize her behavior, her attraction, nor the rejection. "He's not gay, no wife or girlfriend, she had convinced herself. So why ain't I good enough?" After her performance, the last thing she wanted to do was face him again.

"Where's my keys?" she asked in a tone with a hint of irritation, but not much.

"I have them. You'll get them in a second. First, I need to know you're sober enough to drive. I don't want your death, or someone else's on my conscience," Mike replied, convinced this was the only logical explanation for such behavior.

"Like you care.... Anyway, I'm not drunk and you've made it clear you don't want me, so just give me my keys so I can go home."

"I never said I didn't want you. You've just got alot going on. I'm used to being the predator and not the prey. I was intimidated."

"Intimidated by me, for what?!"

"Well, for starters, I'm probably old enough to be your father. I just came home from prison and haven't touched a woman in a long time. You're beautiful, independent... That's a lot for a brother to take in all at once, plus you're sassy."

She smiled from ear to ear. Honesty was not something heard often in her life, or line of business. It had been so long since she'd met a man of substance that she hadn't realized just how much it was needed, or how good it felt.

"Can I get a "do over?" Hi, my name is Cora. If you don't have plans when you get off work, I'd like to take you to the waffle house, your treat?" she said with a bashful smile.

"I have about forty-five minutes before my shift ends and someone comes to relieve me. If you don't mind waiting, or would like to come back and pick me up... I'd love to treat you," Mike said as he returned from behind the counter and began restocking and rearranging merchandise.

"Tell you what. By the time I walk to my car in these god-awful heels that have been killing my feet all night, then pull into traffic and think of a destination other than home. Your shift will be over. Soooo... How about I get comfortable and hang around here, then we leave together?" Cora suggested after taking off both shoes and placing them on the counter with an exhausted loud plop.

"I suppose that will be all right. You know what I do, now what kind of work do you do?" Mike asked while using a pricing gun to place red stickers on the row of orange juice in the see-through glass door freezer.

Cora felt like a little girl blushing over liking a boy. This was the first time in a long time she was ashamed to tell someone, especially a man, her profession. Most men assumed automatically she was a hoe, a stripper, or both. Although this always enraged her, she knew that was merely denial and guilt. "I'm a stripper. I'm not going to paint a pretty picture like a lot of them do. I've done things I'm not proud of, in and out of the clubs for money," she confessed with tears in her eyes, and shame in her voice.

"Who am I to judge you? I've been locked up the majority of my life."

CHAPTER EIGHTEEN

2014

THE ALL WHITE 2012 MERCEDES Benz SL500, a two-door hardtop convertible, came with soft black leather interior that summoned immediate attention. The ride from work was so exhilarating that like a kid he wanted to yell, again, again!

"You were mighty quiet on the ride here. Is everything alright? I hope my driving ain't it. I tried to take it easy on ya," Cora said with a smile.

"Everything is fine. You gotta remember, only white folks and schools had computers the last time I was on the streets. We're driving around with one in your dashboard. I will say this ride is so smooth it almost put me to sleep. Watching you answer phone calls, turn the music up or down, select songs or radio stations, and all of that while a map shows where we are going without taking your hands off the steering wheel... I'm not even going to touch the hot and cold seats," Mike confessed.

"Awwww. I got you baby. Technology changes so much every six months that someone is always putting me up on the latest must have, or must know, so I can only imagine. Don't get me started bout these iPhone verses Android cellphones.... after 37 years. You got any pussy since you been home?"

Championship

The huge yellow sign with bold black lettering signaled that they had arrived at the Waffle House. Except for bar stools around a long counter in the middle of the establishment, the seating was all booths with salt and pepper shakers, napkins, syrup, and paper menus on the tables.

A grill could be clearly seen sizzling with eggs, turkey, and hash browns. The sweet aroma escaping the waffle maker as soon as the cook opened the handle was intoxicating.

"How was your food?" Cora asked while picking through her eggs daintly.

"Mmmm hmm," was all he could muster as all his senses were being tested at once.

Cora relaxed against the hard backing of the booth and enjoyed watching her guest. She would never admit it to him, herself, or anyone else, but he had somehow reminded her that settling down was a wonderful thing with the right person. Her childhood was filled with molestation, rape, abuse, incest and countless other disappointments that warped her sense of a woman's worth, as well as a man's. Men convinced her that delivering their sexual fantasies was her only purpose in life, and women had convinced her that a man's only purpose was to provide monetary whims by being strung along with sexual promises.

"Why are you staring at me like that?" Mike asked self-consciously before wiping his mouth with a napkin.

"No reason, just enjoying all of this. It's been a while since I have enjoyed some good interesting company. I'm going to have to take you to some of my favorite spots to eat. Yeah.. We're going to do a lot of exploring of your taste buds," she said with a mischievous smile.

Mike reached across the table and grabbed both of her hands. He gently caressed them before looking deeply into her eyes. "You're beautiful, but beautiful women come a dime a dozen. It's like makeup, it can be erased. I want to know about your dreams, goals, and ambitions. I am probably the first man not interested in your sexual prowess... Well correction... at least not this early in the game. We still don't know anything about each other except jobs and that Waffle House is a must have to add. Did I say that right?" He asked unsure.

"No, but it was cute, you tried so it works.... you're something else. You are right about one thing though… you are the first man not interested in whatever that word was, or mean… I call it pussy, and you never told me if you've had some or not since you got home?"

"Prowess. It means unique skill, and no, I haven't."

*

"So what cha tryna get into?" Cora asked Mike as she rolled up one of the blunts purchased from him earlier.

"What else is there to get into this time of night?"

Cora licked the blunt seductively before running the flame of a clear plastic Bic lighter along its length briefly to dry it. She then placed the tip between her lips and lit the opposite end. Cora waited until the roof folded completely back before taking a deep pull of exotic weed into her lungs, holding in the smoke as long as possible, then exhaling.

"The only thing open this time of night is 7-11 and legs... you tryna hit this shit nigga?" she asked while entering the interstate ramp.

Mike reached down into the plastic bag resting on the backseat he'd given her earlier and grabbed the pack of Newports. He tapped the pack against the leather armrest to pack the tobacco inside. The menthol gave him a head-rush, coupled with the cool night's breeze, and light constantly darting in and out of the dark cockpit by the overhead highway street lamps. "You know I can't hit that. I'm on parole. I used to smoke those - they're too strong. I smoke Black and Mild. You should try them."

*

The old two story house sitting off the corner of Birdneck Road and Beautiful Street was built in the early 1900's and appeared to be one story. It sat a quarter mile off the main road with a huge oak tree directly in front of it to the left. A large ditch with only a car width between it and the side of the house,ran the property's length. Bushes, crabapple trees, various shrubberies and a garden were found throughout the five acre lot. The house had a small study, living room, den, small kitchen, studio type bedroom and bathroom upstairs.

Every 10x12 board suppling the outside facing had old faded white paint on them that were either cracking, missing sections of paint, or rotted with gaps that allowed temperature to both invade and escape the structure. Insulation wasn't used at the time of its construction so the summer required several fans, and the winter plenty of heaters.

The scenery was perfect for the isolated feel needed for a movie industry horror film site.... The fact someone had died inside added to this mystique.

The front Xeon blue headlights slowly pierced the darkness ahead, inch by inch, as multiple insects danced around inside each beam attracted to the lights.

The low soothing growl emitted from the engine came to an abrupt stop as she pushed the start/stop engine button on the dashboard. "What's the story here? I swear I couldn't live here... it looks so spooky," Cora admitted as she finished the blunt and stared at what little could be seen from the illumination of both headlights.

"Basically as you see, it was built at a time where there were no building codes or the codes back then were so far behind the codes we have today. The house is around 50 years old. I am currently renovating it to meet today's code. Redoing the installation, putting in new windows, new wiring, new electrical sockets, new appliances, new bathroom, etc." Mike explained even though he was convinced she had no interest whatsoever in the particulars of the history of the house.

"Where you learn about all that. I mean how to work on a house and stuff?"

"While I was locked up I learned just about everything there is to know about houses, cars and small engines like lawn mowers.

"Let's go inside, I want to see."

For the first time in a long time Mike was ashamed. He knew from the beginning of the journey he was out of his league. Their date had allowed him to escape his somber reality and take a small peek into what seemed to be alongside Alice, from the story of Alice in Wonderland.

Mike was well aware of the fact that he had very little to offer coming into the situation but figured he'd enjoy the ride as long as he could. As a man with pride, inviting her into the remnants of his domain constituted a possible deal-breaker. "It's still a work in progress. Basically it's a construction site, and you're not dressed properly. We wouldn't want you to get a nail, or a splinter now, would we?" Mike said, playing to his lovable charm and wit.

"Don't be silly. Stop stalling. Either you invite me in or I'm going in," she stated before plucking blunt ashes over the driver side door.

"Give me a minute to move a few things out of the way and I'll come back and get you." Mike slowly made noises on the way to closing the gap between the car and front door, making sure to give any snakes ample time to escape his path.

The old screen door with missing screen mesh at the top and bottom had a long flimsy spring that caused the door to slap the door frame hard if not carefully closed. He quickly pulled the long string in the middle of the first room to cut on the light. The next thing he did was hide the stack of porn DVDs, and refill the kerosene heater before turning up the heat. Mike grabbed a few tools and gallons of paint, storing them in the first room.

"It's creepy as shit out there. How long did you expect me to wait?" Cora asked while making her way to the all black futon with cedarwood armrest, as she picked up the TV remote.

"I was coming. First, I wanted to clean up a little bit."

Cora looked around at the room she was in. Most of the walls were missing except wood framing with old frayed wire connecting to a socket, or running through the frame. Other sections had wooden slats between the framing, with sections covered in patches of plaster with large chunks missing. The two windows in the room set in the same framing with large thick blankets draped across them, and were held up by two large nails, one nail over each corner of the window frame.

A small glass coffee table set between the futon and 55-inch RCA LED TV that hung on the wall. The elongated kerosene heater was positioned in between the front door but just in front of two french-style doors. A large set of stairs started at the base of the four and a half inch thick door Mike had just drug shut, and swirled over her head without any trace of a handrail ever existing.

"I see somebody has been here working on more than the house," Cora said before giggling and turning up the volume to the Blu-ray porn DVD Mike had forgotten was still in the player.

"Okay, so I watch the occasional fuck flick, who doesn't, now turn it off."

"I don't think so. You got some exclusive shit I haven't even seen, and I have quite an extensive collection," Cora challenged with a devilish grin before making sure to gain his attention while seductively parting her legs and rubbing the moist spot forming in the crotch of her pretty black laced thong.

*

Mike stood in the front doorway waving goodbye at the headlights of the Mercedes as it slowly eased back down the path of his property. He could only shake his head as he thought about the heavy kissing and rubbing that almost caused him to give into her irresistible advances. Blue balls was certainly one rub away.

"What am I doing? She practically raped me in here and I want to. What was that?" Mike slowly pushed the large thick door open to the next room to investigate a sound of something moving around. Before his eyes could adjust to the darkness well enough to see the long pull string to cut the light on in the middle of the room, he noticed a narrow stream of light seeping from the old style ice box which could only be opened by a horizontal handle that actually unlocked it. "Who's in here? Come out before I have to look for you. I promise it won't be pretty. I know you're in here." After a few minutes passed of staring in different directions, he convinced himself that no one was there before closing an old Frigidaire. "Shit. I probably forgot to close it all the way."

"I'm sorry, Mr. I was hungry. Please don't hurt me," a timid voice quivered from somewhere inside the darkness.

CHAPTER NINETEEN

THE PHYSICAL TOLL OF WORRY and sleep deprivation could clearly be seen in both of Nicole's eyes, as well as from the dark circles beneath each of them. Nicole had lost at least five pounds, which she only vaguely noticed because of the unusually loose fit from a pair of jeans that she accidentally wore in the daze of following her normal routine. The jeans were much too tight and had been set aside for charity for months but hadn't been boxed up yet because more important things had taken precedence. "Well, I'll be damn... Now I see why everyone has been asking have I ate, or coaxing me to at least nibble on this or that... Get it together girl... Get it together."

She had been reduced to aimlessly wandering around the apartment until the house phone, or her cellphone rang and provided a possible answer on the other end that would relieve her current condition.

"Knock, knock!"

"Yes, who is it?" she asked after looking through the peephole at an unfamiliar face that caused tears to flow suddenly because of her fear of the deliverance of bad news.

As expected, her tears flowed without any foreseeable restraint. The news delivered by the stranger was received through the crack of the door without any further words being exchanged.

*

"Are you alright? Do you know where you are, or what just happened?"

Nicole could hear the strange voice but was unable to focus on where it came from or who it was. She began to search her memory for some point of familiarity from which she could work her way back.

The last thing she remembered was answering the front door and...

"I'm going to help you up, okay? Nice and slow... easy does it."

The door closing and the sound of the deadbolt being engaged was heard in the far distance. Nicole tried to figure out who it was, or if the unknown male's voice was with her. Both legs struggled to stand, then hold her weight, walking would be a whole other ordeal.

"Here... have some water... you fainted. I just want you to stay calm while I talk to the emergency room operator on the phone to make sure you don't have a concussion, if she will take me off hold."

"Mary… is that you, baby, where have you been?" Nicole could hear herself asking as the woozy feeling and swirls of images became more bizarre. She felt a gentle hand stroke slowly rubbing her back in small, slow soothing circles.

"Yes it's me, momma."

Nicole knew she was dead or in a coma. No logical thought could explain, after searching for her daughter for seventy two hours, she somehow magically appeared.

"Ms. Smith… my name is Mike. I found your daughter in my home. After she explained what happened, I brought her straight here. I can't imagine what you must be going though," Mike explained in a concerned but calming tone.

"I'm so sorry, sir. Do I owe you for any damages? What time is it by the way?" Nicole asked before straightening out her hair and smoothing out her clothing.

"Three thirty in the morning, and don't worry about any damages."

"Well, I'm sure you two have plenty to talk about. So I'm going to go because I work in the evenings and have to get as much sleep as possible. It was nice to meet you. Wish it were under better circumstances. Mary, remember what we talked about. Goodbye Ms. Smith," Mike said before leaving.

Nicole watched as Mike locked and closed the front door of her apartment behind him. She peeked through the cheap white aluminum blinds that came with the apartment unit. Nicole watched his stroll, well, after he'd made a left turn on Birdneck Road, and vanished from her line of sight. She knew this was all done to avoid and prolong speaking with her daughter. Now that they were together, Nicole was furious but knew the situation required delicacy. If Mary ran away without her being angry the way she was now, revisiting the miserable last three days was inevitable, if she relayed any of her present thoughts.

"Are you hungry?"

"No"

"Have you eaten? Are you hurt?"

"No I'm fine… just tired," Mary replied in a timid voice.

"Okay… guess I'll see you in the morning then," Nicole said, unsure if anything else should be talked about.

"Okay, mommy… I'm sorry that I worried you," Mary said before briefly hugging her mother.

"That's okay baby… we'll talk about it in the morning. Now go get your rest while I call your grandma and let her know you're home safe. You know the story with my mother, so this dug up all those fears with her."

*

Mary yawned, stretched, then rolled over, placing a pillow over her head to block out the annoying sunrays wrestling her from sleep. After a few more tosses and turns, it was obvious further sleep was refusing to cooperate. She laid still and listened for any signs that would tell whether or not her mother had gone to work. Mary eased out of bed barefooted in a yellow Spongebob nightgown. She tiptoed past her mother's room and peeked in that direction, only to find the room closed. Mary hurried into the kitchen and poured a large bowl of Fruity Pebbles cereal and milk. The task of cleaning her teeth with braces was bad enough without eating Fruity Pebbles, which the orthodontist had instructed against.

"I see someone has forgotten the last time the orthodontist adjusted those braces and found particles in places only reachable when adjusting them. He specifically said no Fruity Pebbles after hearing a lot of foods you had eaten that could have possibly been the cause," Nicole politely reminded Mary, well aware that she remembered the incident as clear as day before pouring the bowl.

"Knock, Knock!"

Nicole looked through the peephole then stepped to the side and let Bradford in.

"Hey Nik. Where was she?"

Nicole shook her head and the bough broke again. Bradford held her and consoled her while Mary stood there watching. "Do you have any idea how much we were all worried about you? I'm not going to pretend to know, or understand the changes a teenager goes through, but your mom, grandma, and I, are always available to listen," Bradford calmly explained while trying to understand the subtle shaking of Nicole's head, before Mary also saw it.

"I might as well say it now... you don't catch on too well, do you? I hadn't decided how to talk about it, so I haven't yet," Nicole explained to Bradford.

Mary's eyes glanced between them before returning her concentration to the almost empty bowl of cereal that now had high milk to cereal ratio, and badly needed a refill. "It's fine, mom, might as well get it over with, besides… I'm interested in hearing what he has to say. Now, you were saying? I'm guessing you were going to lecture me about running away. Seeing as though you are an expert, I want to hear you explain thirteen years of running away. Oh yeah, mom, by the way, I saw Larry before he died and he told me everything," Mary said with baiting sarcasm dripping from every word as tears drenched her face.

Bradford sat motionless while he tried to make sense of what Mary had just said. He finally chalked it all up as something a mother had discussed about their past relationship when they were both younger, that had been somehow misconstrued in her young mind until he saw Nicole's face drained of color with tears in her eyes.

"Oh my god, Mary... I'm so sorry... You were never supposed to... He shouldn't have told you... He had no right. It wasn't his place damn it!" Nicole whimpered while slowly moving towards her daughter.

"What's wrong... I don't understand… can somebody please just tell me what's going on?" Bradford asked, bewildered. Nicole embraced Mary and slowly comforted her while her body shook uncontrollably in her mother's arms.

"I know baby... that's it... just let it all out. I wish you had come to me instead of running away. We could have worked through this together."

Bradford sat in complete silence while both mother and daughter consoled each other. Unable to fully grasp the situation, but still feeling helpless, he hugged them both. "It's going to be alright."

"Have a seat, both of you, please. Let me go into the kitchen and fix us chamomile tea, it's supposed to be good for relaxation. Take all the time you need. I will handle any affairs you need me to. I was actually planning to tell you both that I'm starting an additional program to work hand in hand with the initial program that started Mary's college program. I'm still trying to work out the bugs and kinks, but basically I will provide rental property for winners of each college fund. I am also planning to help single mothers' purchase properties, cars, and will offer special incentives to based on income participants. I would like the both of you to give me as much input as you can, at a price of course. You would be my personal advisors for lack of a better word. My men on the ground, sort of speaking. What do you say?" Bradford finished with a smile.

"Brad, sit down," Nicole said calmly.

"No thank you, I'm fine."

"Brad, sit down!"

"Ok, ok,a little too enthusiastic but..."

"Mary's your daughter... that's what this is all about."

Bradford sat down promptly without a word searching for the right words in his head to say. "My daughter? how, I mean... well, I guess I know how... but when, are you sure?" Bradford asked with confusion and uncertainty apparent in his voice.

"Remember you came home, candlelight, lobster tail, white wine... spare no expense? You still don't catch on to hints, do you?"

"Y'all must not of used a rubber, cause my mom's trying to talk around me again like I'm slow or some little kid," Mary interrupted.

Both Bradford and Nicole fell silent and looked at Mary, realizing for the first time she was no longer the innocent little girl they still wanted her to be.

"As far as being sure, yeah I'm sure. We can take a paternity test if you want though, it's up to you," Nicole said with a carefree air about her.

"That won't be necessary... why? Did you think I wouldn't be a good father? Why?" Bradford whispered.

"I don't know. I wanted to tell you but I started to think maybe you were doing so well and I ran into Sabrina one day, and when she saw Mary, she knew..."

"She kept trying until I told her and swore her to secrecy. The only way she agreed not to tell you was allowing her to set up a monthly allowance, hence the college fund story. Sabrina has tried to get me to contact you over the years but grew more persistent lately. Next thing I know, I come home and you're in my apartment. Imagine the surprise I received. I thought you knew and had told Mary then," Nicole explained with exhaustion.

"All of that is in the past, Mary. Larry and I had an estranged relationship but I have always respected him. I think I kind of always thought we had plenty of time to sort things out between us. I never ran away from you. I could never do such a thing, and I won't right now. There's obviously a lot of hurt, mistrust, fear and a lot of other emotions and feelings going on between us. I'm hoping we can all start over again and become a family. What do you both say to that idea?" Bradford proposed.

"I'm willing to consider it..."Nicole trailed off.

"Promise not to make my mother cry ever again and we might have a deal," Mary instructed.

"I promise!"

CHAPTER TWENTY

THE REFLECTION IN THE REAR view mirror revealed slight dark areas contrasting beautifully with the smokey eye shadow make-up. She could still distinguish the two. "Babygirl, it wouldn't hurt to not say anything sometimes. You're killing me with the truth," Nicole rhetorically stated to the mirror before the light turned green, allowing her to pull into the Exxon gas station by her house.

"Ms. Smith? I thought that was you, how are you?"

Nicole couldn't quite see the face of a large man approaching her because of the sun's brightness shining at her face from behind him.

"Who's that? I can't see," she calmly said after pushing the automatic door lock button, raising all four windows, except for a crack's width, enough for words to slip in and out of, then pushing the passenger seat's visor so that it swung out and covered the top half of the doorway, blocking the sun from her face.

"I'm sorry, it's me. Mike, from the other night. I work here. Would you like me to pump your gas?"

"Oh no, that won't be necessary. I can do it. I wanted to thank you for making sure my daughter got home safely, but so much has been going on since then I haven't had time to get your address from her, to come by and thank you in person."

"No need to thank me, just doing my civic duty," Mike said as he signaled the cashier to turn on the pump, pushed open the gas door, and began fueling her vehicle. "Nice Altima."

"Thanks, by the way. Do you have any idea why my daughter broke into your house? I mean... there's no good reason to break into anyone's home. I guess what I'm asking is, do you have any idea why your home?" Nicole asked after lowering her window.

"She said her grandmother used to stay in the house I live in. I explained my mother and her grandfather's mother were best friends. Mrs. Garrett left the house to my mother in her will because her son... well, you know the rest."

"No, I don't; no one would tell me," Nicole stressed with tears in both eyes.

"So, you know Gertrude, huh?" Nicole shook her head and laughed at the thought.

"Who?" asked Mike

"My mother, Gertrude."

"No, I'm sorry, I was talking about your real mother Vanessa, your father Shawn, and his mother Annie Garrett, my late mother's best friend."

Nicole had concluded a long day at work and could only envision a nice hot shower, nap, cooking dinner, then and only then, mentally returning to the subject of Bradford being Mary's father. A quick routine stop by the gas station was necessary to prevent the need to stop for at least another two weeks. The names she'd just heard had siphoned the air from her lungs.

"You know my mother and father... how?" she asked as both her shoulders relaxed before she gave her undivided attention.

Mike stood staring at her for a moment before a wave of compassion passed over him. He opened the passenger door and nervously slipped inside. Nicole started the car and buckled up until she was parked in the employee parking space right in front of the Exxon gas station.

"Don't worry about me. I need to know everything about my parents. All these years my grandma has refused to tell me. As I grew older I decided that digging up the past might kill her. She lost her only daughter and raised her only granddaughter as her daughter... just tell me everything."

"You're the spitting image of your mother Vanessa. She was beautiful. I met her working at Mcdonalds not long after I'd moved down here from Washington D.C. I can still see her unforgettable smile. Anyway, I was in love with her. I fell in love with her the first time I laid eyes on her. I was working at the Sundial motel cleaning rooms at the time. I was getting into a lot of trouble in the city so I moved down here with my mom. God rest her soul. I was head over heels, late for work, couldn't sleep, and all of that. Your grandmother Gertrude wanted to meet me, but Vanessa wasn't ready to introduce us so we snuck around. I ended up going back to the city and she begged me not to go. I stayed a little longer than expected. When I came back into town I stopped by her job and saw her holding hands with this guy. She came from behind the counter and I saw she was pregnant. I left without her noticing me and later that night got drunk and killed a man in a fit of rage at a bar at the oceanfront. Racism was a lot worse then than it is now, because he was white I served thirty seven years of my life behind bars," Mike confessed while clenching his fists and staring off into space.

Nicole tried to sort every piece of information then reposition it so that it all made sense. It was obvious he loved her mother deeply. If she were to believe him, her mother loved him as well. Women didn't just love a man one minute and then turn around and become pregnant by another man in a blink of an eye. Nicole knew that the story was void of several key pieces she needed. "Mike, if you know my father, where did you two know each other from?"

"I found out the same year I was going to trial, your mother had been killed. It was a crime of passion. It wasn't until my mother came to see me and asked that I look out for her best friend's son if I came across him, that I figured out he was the guy I'd seen with her that day. He was placed in the hole and refused to be moved to general population. His trial took a lot of the focus off my trial. At the time, I began to have nightmares in which I would wake up in cold sweats with tears streaming down my face, apologizing to your mother. I was convinced maybe if I had approached them that day things could have turned out differently."

"That's too much to carry around on your heart. I don't know why things happen the way they do, but I've got to believe God has a bigger plan for us all."

"I wouldn't have believed that except after being tormented by these demons for over twenty years, one day they suddenly stopped, the same day my celly Red confided in me the crime he had committed... he was your father Shawn. I beat him until he was unrecognizable for what he'd done to your mother!" Mike said with death in his eyes.

"Did he tell you why he did it?" Nicole let the words slip out, never really wanting Mike to have the answer, for fear it would crush the fragile pieces of what was left, holding her life together.

"No I didn't even ask. I think knowing would have tormented me to this very day. I needed closure, not another door opened so I..."

Nicole said everything with a compassion in her eyes that her mouth could never be encouraged to say. Regardless of what Shawn had done, he was still responsible for her existence. Even though he had killed her mother, Nicole had conflicting feelings about the man beside her revealing he had hurt her father. Confusion pulled her loyalty, anger, sympathy, and thoughts in various directions. "I need you to get out of my car. Thank you for telling me what happened. You have to understand this has all been an open wound that has never been discussed so I have been unable to heal from it. Now time must take its course."

"I understand. You know where I work and live, if you ever have any more questions."

Nicole waited for Mike to exit the car and make the same turn onto Birdneck he'd made the morning he showed up on her doorstep with her missing child. Each low deep sob was overpowered by the thought of his presence happening to be involved in both situations, her daughter missing, and the truth about her father. The problem being, she'd never been one to give into the possibility of coincidences, and wasn't going to start now. Nicole started babygirl and drove through the parking lot behind the gas station which consisted of a Food Lion, chinese store, Subway, laundry mat, Long John Silvers, and a neighborhood barber shop called Premiers.

"Lord, why me? I know you said you wouldn't put on us any more than we can handle but this, my mother's death, father sentenced to life, my daughter and her father, and this guy showing up in the midst of everything. The past is really coming back to haunt me and I don't know why?"

Traffic allowed her to make it home safely. She sat in front of the apartment and tried to pull herself together as best she could. Once she exited the car and put the front door key in the lock, she took a deep breath to prepare for whatever lay on the other side before opening it.

"Mary, I'm home, baby, how was your day?"

CHAPTER TWENTY-ONE

"YOU KNOW YOU SHOULD HAVE told me. We go back… since grade school, Brina."

"What can I say? It wasn't my place so I pressed her, and when that didn't work, I came up with that little stupid guest speaker engagement to bring y'all together," Sabrina responded casually over her shoulder to Bradford's mild expression of hurt while thumbing through jean sizes on a round metal clothing display rack.

"What do you think about these? True religion to these kids is like Armani and Tom Ford tailored fit suits are to you."

The Macy's department store in Lynnhaven Mall was crawling with shoppers. Some were cutting through the store to enter the actual mall, others were browsing or taking advantage of the savings offers in the Virginian-Pilot's Sunday newspaper advertisements. Bradford was clearly out of place. Not only was his shopping usually done online, or by Sabrina without his presence, but he was now in the women's department. He had decided Mary would be dragging him there sooner or later so why not get all of his anxiety out of the way.

"Okay, Brad, let's go pick up a few pairs of bras and panties."

*

Several Macy's shopping bags with the vibrant red Macy's star were juggled as Brad tried not to drop one. Keeping an eye on Sabrina, as she darted through droves of shoppers and out into the huge parking lot, was far more than he bargained for.

"Wait right here while I pull the car around. Awww, daddy's little girl is going to be so cute in those outfits," Sabrina said before spinning around and dropping a huge pair of black Gucci shades over her eyes. She stretched every thread of the black skin tight, backless, tight dress that clearly revealed she didn't have any panties on with each and every step of her bouncy strut.

"Why didn't you get this?" Brad asked with a look of disgust on his face while walking to the front of the vehicle, only to be directed to the trunk to store the shopping bags. "Porsche is not front wheel drive, nor does the trunk belong in the rear. What is a Macon turbo anyway?"

"Oh hush. It's all wheel drive, has room for five, 0 to 60 in 4.2 seconds, and averages 19 miles per gallon. With all that in an SUV, I'm thinking maybe a first car for Mary. Daddy?"

"I see you will be working with Nicole and Mary against me, instead of with me," Bradford said after realizing he was helpless in the situation.

The ride back through the old neighborhood was therapeutic. Bradford remembered how rough it was growing up under Monica's roof, especially now after experiencing having a child of his own. Mary being the opposite sex allowed him to see how challenging it must have been for his mother raising him. It made him appreciate her sacrifices a little more.

Sabrina pulled the car into the second court parking lot of Atlantis apartments and stopped perpendicular to Nicole's Altima. This made Brad nervous because Sabrina not looking for a parking space meant she was leaving him with two unpredictable females to deal with by himself.

"And where do you think you're going? You expect me to carry all of these bags again? You could have at least parked closer, Sabrina."

"What's up with this Sabrina shit? Plus, all that working out you do... Put your back into it," Sabrina teased while patting his left shoulder, releasing the tailgate, and playfully giggling at the same time.

Bradford got out of the car and looped as many bags as he could around each arm and hand before grabbing a few with his mouth. He used an elbow to bring the tailgate back down low enough to close it with his fist.

"Sure I can't offer any help?" Sabrina lightly taunted as he fumbled with trying to get the hallway door open with both arms and hands full.

Bradford stumbled into the hallway and helplessly just kept slightly throwing himself against the front door. Finally, he saw the peephole darken from inside.

"Hey Brad... And what on earth is all this?" Nicole asked before placing both hands on her hips and trying to take in all that stood before her in the doorway. "Well, don't just stand here looking like an overdressed bellhop. Come on in, silly. Take all of that straight back, the first door you see is Mary's."

"And these are for you," Bradford said in a hospitable tone that piggybacked off her bellhop statement before handing her a few bags.

"Chanel Number 5, Fashion Fair Cosmetics makeup, Coach bag, Prada, Marc Jacobs, Ives Saint Laurent, and Victoria's Secret lingerie... You give new meaning to the term I come bearing gifts. I don't know what to say, Brad. I'm at a loss for words," Nicole nervously rambled.

"I'm glad you like it. There should be a few gift cards and I left the receipts inside the bags in case you or Mary want another color, style, or something doesn't fit. I hope I didn't overstep any boundaries with the lingerie," Bradford said earnestly.

"Like it! I love it! And as for the lingerie, that's fine. I needed some new panties and bras. I had no urgency because it's been awhile since I've been able to entertain a man in that manner. What? I'm just being honest... oh get over yourself, boy. I'm yo baby momma now," Nicole teased, knowing Bradford hated when she used what he called ghetto talk.

"Speaking of baby mama, where is Mary?" I noticed she wasn't in her room.

"You mean your daughter, right? Get used to calling her your daughter. Anyway, I let her go with her friends since I've been keeping her butt cooped up for the last couple of weeks. I haven't seen what you got her but I'm sure she's going to love it. It says female sales clerk, or Sabrina written all over it," Nicole revealed with a warm smile.

"So, you're saying I'm incapable of shopping and picking items such as what you hold in your hands?"

"Okay, Brad. How did your mother respond to the news of you having a child?" Nicole asked, side-stepping the light banter and finally tackling one of the many elephants crowding the room.

"It's complicated. You know we don't have the warmest of relationships. She's excited about seeing you and Mary. My fault, my daughter. I just don't think it's time yet. My mother has a lot to digest so I want to build a bond of trust with Mary before I introduce the two of them. Of course, this doesn't sit well with my mother at all. She's sixty-nine and living alone in a 3-bedroom house and working long hours to keep busy, so basically she's lonely. Trust me. I'm going to make it happen."

"I feel sorry for Monica. Your father was the love of her life. When he died she poured all of her love and attention into you, not realizing she not only smothered you but the relationship as well. A big part of the reason I never told you about Mary is I didn't want your mother's strong presence affecting the choices I decided to make in raising our child."

"I don't know how to respond to that. I still wish you had told me. The good thing is it's never too late. How's my little girl been dealing with all this considering that she's known for quite some time before revealing it to the both of us?"

"Little girl? She's anything but that. I think she's fine with it all though. She asks me questions about you out of the blue, or tells me she's going to ask you for this or that. I'm focusing on having you two build a strong relationship, not having a man in her life that she sees maybe once a month that brings gifts out of guilt. I don't want her manipulating that guilt to get things she wants either."

"I didn't buy those gifts out of guilt. Neither of you can expect me to up and move here either. This is all new to me, but I promise to do the very best I know how."

"I know your gifts aren't out of guilt. I also don't expect you to just drop everything and come running. I'm sorry if I somehow gave you that impression. We've been fine all this time, but she's getting older and no matter how good the years have been for my denial, the fact remains that a girl needs her father. She needs you. Only a father can teach his daughter how a man should treat her. She doesn't understand you can't drop everything for her. She's still a child, Brad. At this age, it's all about what she wants. The upside to that is that she wants time with you."

The weight of Nicole's words was like a ton of bricks weighing on Bradford's mind. "Well, for starters, this new nonprofit idea will require my attention in this area. Maybe we can look for a house not too far from here and take it from there. Something tells me Sabrina might be signing a lease or loan agreement as we speak because she was so secretive about where she was going when she dropped me off."

"My lips are sealed. Sabrina is a really good friend to both of us. I actually used to be jealous of the relationship the two of you have. Even had the silly notion you slept together," Nicole said before laughing.

"So what's been going on new with you lately?" Bradford asked to keep from having a conversation that could end up becoming a problem.

Nicole recognized the sudden change in the subject and found it peculiar. She made a note of it in her mental Rolodex to bring up at a more opportune time. "Well, I found out the guy who returned our daughter safely knew my mother and father. I was curious as to why Mary chose his house but in all the excitement, I never got around to asking. Apparently he had a thing for my mother and met my father in prison while doing 30 something years and just recently got out," Nicole said, still mentally questioning Bradford's reasoning for changing the subject.

Sarcasm or some other form of expression borrowed from the female tool box filled with Mmm's, Mmm Hmm's, eye rolling, hand clapping, finger snapping, lip smacking, or the infamous neck roll were clearly present, but why? Was the thing that had him confused. "I'd like to meet him in person. Maybe I can help him out in some way. It can't be easy coming home in this rough economy."

"That would be nice, it's worth a shot. He works at the Exxon on the corner but I seem to recall offering him money for any damages Mary may have caused breaking in his house and he declined. Later when I asked Mary, she said the house was dilapidated but upon further examination, he was renovating."

"Time really does fly when you're having fun. I really enjoyed your hospitality, Nik. But it's getting late, no telling where Brina is, right."

Nicole crossed the room and stopped any further sound from exiting his mouth with her tongue. Bradford was caught off guard looking at his Franck Muller timepiece at the precise instant she kissed him. Nicole softly massaged his hand in hers before pulling him slowly towards her bedroom.

"Are you sure Nik? I mean... Things are already complicated."

She smiled as the moistness between her legs came as a direct response to his usage of the name Nik. She merely stared back into his eyes with a look of hunger and lust before taking his index finger into her mouth sensually then slowly disappearing into her bedroom door. "Oooh Braaaad!"

Before Brad could completely break the door jamb's threshold, Nicole attacked him with her mouth and hands. The huge floral comforter was all he saw before being tossed on top of it. Like wild animals they pulled, tugged, and then ripped off every inch of clothing that refused to surrender to their desires.

"Nik… Ahhhh… your body is so beautiful and firm," Bradford confessed in the heat of passion as he held both firm breasts and traced his tongue over each anticipatory nipple.

"Yes… Oh yes. Right there," Nicole moaned with her head thrown back and gripping the back of his head as he skillfully expressed his missing her.

Bradford swung her around and climbed on top of her briefly, making eye contact that signaled the intensity of his next move.

"No… Okay… Okay! I can't take no more, please Brad. Come up here, please. Put it in," Nicole whined as several convulsions rendered her body helpless. Sleep overcame them both after hours of passionate lovemaking without a hint of its presence. Brad felt Nicole steering and rolled over to investigate a possible second bout.

"Oh my God, Mom? Brad?" Mary blurted out in shock before backing away from the scene unfolding before her very eyes in her mother's bedroom.

CHAPTER TWENTY-TWO

One year later....

THE MOUTH WATERING SMELL OF brown-N-serve rolls could easily be identified even though they were securely wrapped in aluminum foil and sitting on top of the stove. String beans, cabbage, Jiffy cornbread, Stovetop Stuffing, homemade potato salad, ham, fruit salad, and cranberry sauce all lined the countertops and dining room table, fighting for aroma supremacy while tarrying for the turkey's first appearance out of the oven.

"Get the pilgrim and Indian placemats out. No, better yet, get the red and green dollies out," Monica requested.

"Ma, calm down. Everything looks and smells great. Ain't that right, Brina?" Bradford said, hoping Sabrina would lend some further serenity to the stressful situation.

"Yeah, uh huh, Monica, everything smells heavenly... off sides!" Sabrina stood up and yelled as a flag was thrown on the Dallas Cowboys, who were playing against the Washington Redskins football team on T.V.

"You ain't no help. You didn't help cook,helping calm my mom... Remind me again, why are you here?" Bradford asked.

"Oh... simple, to eat, and cuz you love me. Now get out the front of the T.V."

*

Monica, Bradford, Cora, Mike, Gertrude, Nicole, Mary, Mildred, and Sabrina all held hands with their heads bowed. The food's presentation was flawless, all that remained was the actual taste.

"Lord, I want to thank you once again for allowing us to assemble with family and friends one more time. I especially want to thank Larry's mother, Mildred, for coming, as well as Sabrina for extending the invitation. I want to thank you for answering my prayers to heal my relationship with my son, and giving me the opportunity to be a better grandmother then I was a mother. After losing Bradford's father I lost a large part of myself, but you've restored it through family. I also want to thank you for bringing Mike into our lives. He is a wonderful gift that keeps on giving to us all. I now want to extend this moment to allow everyone to say exactly what it is they are thankful for," Monica said with a smile and tears of joy in both eyes.

"I'm thankful for change and placing such a lovely young lady in my life," Mike said with a smile.

"I'm thankful for my engagement, and meeting a man that not only introduced me to self love but showed me how to find it," Cora explained with misty eyes while making sure everyone saw her three carat princess cut canary diamond in a platinum setting.

"I want to thank God for giving me health and strength at my age. I also want to thank God for my family, and Monica for having us in her lovely home," Gertrude said.

"I want to thank God for my mom, my dad, my two grandmas and most of all those stupid braces coming off so I can really dig in this year," Mary said before everyone started laughing.

"I want to thank God for answering my prayers and allowing a second chance to get it right," Nicole said as she shed a few tears. She squeezed her mother's and daughter's hand before mouthing 'I love you so much' to Brad.

"I want to thank God for still being in the land of the living. At one point, losing my son meant I lost the will to live. I am so thankful that Sabrina stayed in contact with me," Mildred confessed.

Sabrina squeezed Mildred's hand lightly as she looked at the ceiling and soft tears flowed down her face. "Lord, thank you for the time we spent with your angel Larry before you called him back home. Thank you for letting us share this wonderful meal as a family... oh, thanks for letting my Cowboys whip them Indians again!" she taunted, knowing Mike was a Redskin fan.

"Okay. I want to thank God for blessing me with success beyond my wildest dreams, then showing me that my daughter, her mother, and a non-profit idea could give me more wealth, happiness, and fulfillment then all of the money in the world. All the money I have doesn't hurt either," Bradford said with a smile and touch of humor.

Everyone passed each dish around the table after expressing thanks, each one taking as much as their eyes convinced their bellies they could consume.

"Don't be shy, there's plenty of Reynolds Wrap, and aluminum foil for to-go plates. I know y'all barely have room for dessert but there is pumpkin pie, apple pie, cherry pie, carrot cake pound cake, red velvet cake, fruit cake, banana pudding, and lemon meringue pie left," Monica offered as everyone hugged and kissed while saying their goodbyes.

"I'm going to stay back and help clean up, baby. Sabrina is going to drop my mom off on her way to drop Mildred off. Of course your spoiled rotten daughter wants to stay as well," Nicole said glowing all over the place.

"When are we going to tell everybody that you're pregnant? You can't hide something like that forever, Nik," Bradford warned.

"I know. I know. I just want to have something that's all ours for a change. Even if it's only for a brief moment," Nicole said, appealing to his sense of privacy. He popped her on the ass and turned around to see his mother staring at the both of them.

"I had a dream about fish swimming the other morning. That means somebody's pregnant. I just took notice of that glow on Nicole. Anyway, ain't none of my business but congratulations. Gotta make a stop real quick. If I ain't back before you leave, lock up, son," Monica said with a smile.

EPILOGUE

Secrecy

THE OLD BROKEN-DOWN TWO-STORY HOUSE built in the 1900's that once sat just off Birdneck Road was no more. In its place stood a cozy red and brick home with black shingles and matching black shutters. The inside was filled with wood flooring, central air and heat, along with all new plumbing, bathroom and kitchen sinks and fixtures, new doors, and a new cast iron wood burning stove. The property was cut and receded, and the huge oak tree out front was pruned.

"Thanks for the ride, Cora," Mike said before kissing her on the cheek and walking towards the front door.

"Want some pussy.... I mean company? No one should be alone on Thanksgiving night, baby."

"Appreciate it. Rain check?"

Mike quickly went inside and tidied up. He knew even though he turned her down, this only made her more persistent. The brake lights' glare became smaller and smaller as the reflection disappeared from the front window pane. He stared at the folded piece of paper sitting next to the half empty bottle of Grey Goose. Mike slowly picked it up then quickly placed it in his back pocket when he heard the familiar sound of an engine approaching. The headlights cut off and he imagined her sexy thick body walking towards the front door.

"Oh babe, my mouth been watering all night long thinking about this moment," she whispered while dropping to her knees with the front door open, proving she was a true exhibitionist.

He grabbed her face, making sure to fill every inch of her mouth while enjoying the texture and shape of each tooth rubbed against in the process. Her firm breasts were released from her bra, but stood at full attention as if they were still being supported.

"Fuck me, Mike! Please… Fuck me!" she enticed.

Mike stepped out of his jeans and watched her soft, huge, wide ass spread as she got down on all fours and spread her asscheeks, allowing her thick moisture to be seen matted between her pussy hairs.

"Am I your bitch? Slap my ass when you fuck me then, baby," she cooed.

Mike mounted her from behind. She bucked and howled as he smack her ass, ramming himself inside her until he collapsed on her back. "I'll be right back. Let me piss and wash off. I'll bring you a soapy rag when I get back," he said.

While he was gone she played with her clit until she noticed a folded piece of paper in the back pocket of his jeans crumpled up on the floor. She went back to priming for the second round of sex but couldn't seem to concentrate because of her curiosity over that piece of paper.

Mike returned with the soapy rag in his hand and dropped it immediately to the floor as soon as he saw the letter in her hand...."Monica.... I can... Let me explain."

"Explain? The letter does all the explaining, in case you are slow in comprehension. Let me read it aloud to make sure I understand. Michael Perry, in the case to determine if Nicole Smith is your biological daughter, the results of the DNA test show 99.78% she is your daughter.... When were you going to tell me? When were you going to tell her for that matter?"

"I.... I haven't decided yet... I literally just found out."

OUTRO

In case you didn't know

IN THE EARLY 1900'S THE names "Little Africa" and "Greenwood" were names given to the area north of the Frisco railroad tracks in Tulsa, Oklahoma by white residents. It became one of the most prominent concentrations of African American businesses in the United States and became popularly known as "Black Wallstreet." The Tulsa race riots of 1921, in which the Oklahoma state government, with the help of Tulsa's white residents, massacred hundreds of black residents and destroyed the neighborhood within hours. This is one of the most devasting massacres in the history of U.S. race relations. I include this history because although Seatack was on a smaller scale, at the exact time on two different coasts, blacks pulled together and not only made lemonade out of lemons, they expanded so far that the government took part in destroying what they created. Seatack has been affected in more subtle ways, such as the use of back tax laws where the owner loses land because of unknown accumulated taxes owed, and imminent domain laws where the government or state has taken land for the construction of highways or power plant easements.

Last but not least, the buying or new management companies in lower income residents that force relocation because of higher rent or extra rental requirements not able to be met by current tenants, such as an income three times the rent to stay after the rent has been raised $3-500 more. This information ties in to my characters because each is not only a resident of Seatack but descendants. The blood of powerful, resilient slaves courses through each house and street of the area, which were once dirt roads, before that swampland. In my innocence I constantly stumbled into bumps, straps, and mistakes swaddled in mischief. I was given an outlet by Ms. Bernadine, shown compassion by Ms. Snead, and mentored by Bubba That my friends is the tenacity, integrity, love, and wholesomeness of the area..... welcome to Seatack, Virginia.

NOW THAT YOU KNOW, WHAT ARE YOU GOING TO DO ABOUT IT TO ENSURE HISTORY DOESN'T CONTINUE TO REPEAT ITSELF?!

AFTERWORD

THE PRESSURE OF COMPLETING THIS particular body of work was Paramount!! I'm unsure whether it is the stickler in me, ignorance concerning the publishing process and its totality, or just good old fashioned healthy critique? I am an introvert exposing my thoughts reluctantly. Representation of many generations before,and after my birth are entangled, snared, woven, and unraveled throughout this literary writing.

After serving his country during World War II Robert Lee and Anna belle Albritton,my grandparents,became loving servants, and pioneers of Seatack, Virginia since the 1900s. In 1943 at age 21 Robert built a structure that housed 10 kids. He later built a house using huge round faced bricks after molding them and cooking them in a kiln before laying each one. They became two out of the three grocery store owners serving the Seatack community naming the store "Sunset Confessionary". In addition to helping Robert sell coal, oil, and various other products. Anna belle offered affordable daycare,and sold her famous potato jacks with only the use of one arm due to a stroke at age 21.She went on to having 7 more children after the doctors diagnosed she would be unable to have any more.

Historical and history are words commonly found in Social Studies and History classes as required core subjects to pass and graduate. Somehow this criteria eluded Seatack's contributions to the American dream. It is the epitome of setting out and accomplishing the intangible amongst a world of sounding brass and tingling cymbals.The strong beat of Seatack's heart, light plucking of your heart strings and whispers from the wind section. One might describe it as a maestro symphony performance by community cohesiveness.

So you see….my dear readers….as I previously stated…pressure.I am a direct descendant of a specific geographical pulse that has beat unwavering for over 100 years. A pulse of African drums and old slave hymns filled with grit, honor loyalty, blood, sweat, tears, pride perseverance, love, truth, empathy, kindness, and, ambition, innovativeness integrity, suffering, resilience, compassion….. Seatack!!!!!!….to my ancestors that came and went before me.I pray this native son has done you all proud.

QUESTIONNAIRE

1. How did Monica's parenting ultimately impact her son?
2. Do you agree or disagree with her methods?
3. Should Bradford have visited Cora at the strip club during his emotional vulnerability?
4. Why did Cora feel ashamed of her profession when telling Michael? What made him, a felon, exempt?
5. Should felons be viewed as lower class citizens or equals?
6. Do you agree with Gertrude's use of the nickname Gerddy?
7. Was Gertrude justified to keep Bradford and Nicole apart?
8. What did you think about all the characters giving thanks together in the end?
9. After all that happened, did Bradford find something priceless back home, or was it always present and rediscovered?
10. Should Michael have been given 45 years for his part in the bar scene?
11. How should racism as a whole, and injustice in the judicial system be handled?
12. Why didn't Nicole tell Bradford immediately about her pregnancy?
13. Do you think Nicole would have ever told him if not confronted by the truth her daughter revealed?
14. Should Sabrina have told Bradford of Nicole's pregnancy? Why do you think she didn't?
15. How do you think Mary now views her mother after knowing the whole truth?

I pray you have enjoyed each character and maybe recognized a similarity in yourself, friend, or family member. We are all flawed and often pass harsh judgement but would do ten times worse if placed in that person's situation. Humble pie does not have to be eaten when you eat empathy, brush and floss three times a day with sympathy. Pride is a terrible thing when used incorrectly. I am the epitome of it. I often say my tail of pride is ten feet tall and twenty foot wide... but I know how to tuck my tail. God bless you all... for I humbly forever remain a work in progress.

Feel free to contact me: MiraculousEvidence@gmail.com, or social media Facebook, Twitter, Snapchat, and Instagram.

Here's an excerpt from my up and coming release. I hope you enjoy it.

Social Butterflies

"It is easy to look and admire another's beauty, lifestyle, and possessions. It is just as easy to cheat, rather than study for a test. Finding the easy way out is the nature of man, it is also the undoing. Be thankful for whatever your situation may be. You have no idea the cost, what it takes to keep, or what others are willing to do to sustain an appearance that is often a facade."

PROLOGUE

"KEEP YOUR HEAD DOWN AND no one will see you, or even know you're there... like usual," she coaxed herself as her eyes rode the grooves of the hard black rubber mat that centered the high school bus aisle. The stop she got on seemed to draw little to no attention. Loud talk, joking and blank stares out of the windows were happening on either side of her "so far so good."

The front seats always allowed a quick squat and even faster escape when the line started to form to exit the bus. A week before, she would wonder what it felt like to ride in the back of the bus with all the popular kids. Coming to terms with the fact that the cards dealt her consisted of being second, or third in life was taken in stride, it was certainly better than last. A peculiar thing, the front seats were filled for the past week, almost as if someone had arranged the seating. She knew that was silly, who'd have such power and use it to place her in the choice backseats? Before she could process this rhetorical question and return to the thought of one more day of paradise, their eyes met.

Miriam white was as "Lily white" as they come. She was stunning from all angles, hair, and flawless skin that sparkled under the dimmest of light..... which was affirmed by her yearbook picture. Bourgeoisie was clearly a word she handed to the doctor just before she stepped out of her mother at birth. She manipulated students and teachers just because. Neil, the junior varsity star quarterback, was more her accessory than the title he held as her boyfriend. When she decided he was no longer exciting she dumped him, and no girl would come within 10 feet of him for fear of her wrath. It was hard to stay off Miriam's radar while she showed off the latest fashions and pointed out the people wearing thrift store clothing and various other irregular fabrics.

Teresa kept a hole somewhere, no matter how hard she tried not to. If it wasn't a run in her knee-high stockings, it was a missing button on a sweater. This forced her to become proficient with a needle and thread, which remained on standby wherever she went. Although Teresa carried a soft countenance with perfect white teeth, those black cat like shaped eyeglasses with the thin chain that kept them from dropping and hung around the back of the neck, killed her confidence.

"Since you keep violating the seating arrangement, you might as well eat lunch with us too." A voice broke Teresa out of her trance just quick enough to see Miriam halfway off the bus. This sudden turn of events made Teresa nervous. She liked Miriam's ex-boyfriend Neil and had been seeing him, well..... sort of. Miriam asked him to meet after school, now Miriam was inviting Teresa to eat at the Round Table... what was she up to?

CHAPTER ONE

Twenty nine years later....

"HAPPY NEW YEARS!" COULD BE heard by various voices screaming in the background as she sat at the massive sized desk, and fondled the old cat like glasses still connected to that same old chain. 2008 meant a New Year to the rest of the world, but to Teresa, it was just another day without the love of her life.

Miriam robbed her of everything and it had all begun 29 years prior. Teresa lost her husband 9 years ago, making her a widow of two beautiful girls ages eight and five at the time. No hobby would fill the void her heart felt. They say "time heals all wounds" ....the intensity hadn't lessened any in 9 years, so when was it supposed to start, she wondered?

After 10 years of legal battles, Teresa won the lawsuit against Miriam; too bad Neil died before the final verdict. Teresa's husband needed a heart transplant that cost $250,000. The multi-million dollar lawsuit was driving them into bankruptcy, placing a strain on their marriage and his heart condition. Teresa knew it was a personal vendetta, the reason Miriam wouldn't lend them the money in the first place.

Against her husband's wishes, she resolved to appeal to whatever human section of heart Miriam had left. "I'll drop the suit if you'll just pay for the transplant and legal fees." Teresa could hear herself pleading as if it were yesterday, as the tears flowed freely down her face. The jewelry and apparel design for Virginia Beach's socialites were all her designs ever since high school.

Miriam had taken undeserved credit for decades. When Teresa created a more affordable line called "The black moth" Miriam claimed it would infringe on the current emblem and Social Butterflies brand. Teresa knew Miriam stole millions, the lawyers produced sales figures from overseas that showed "The black moth" was an exclusive high-end collection sold throughout Eastern Europe. Teresa made her peace years ago. Miriam had the money and she had happiness, she had Neil. Now he was gone, her happiness was in jeopardy... she needed help.....

Teresa hired a team of advisors and won everything. She allowed Miriam to remain the face of the company. Miriam was left broke with a six-figure salary. Teresa considered this more than generous, all things considered.

Teresa looked at the check she just got in the mail a few days ago and decided it should be used to retain a team of good lawyers. She loaded the revolver and placed it in her purse. "Today we even the score, Miriam," she whispered before she made sure to remember the exact time.

DEDICATIONS

TO JAMES EDMONDS MY DAD, you are the true definition of the meek inheriting the Earth. Uncle Tyrone, we may not see each other often but you are still my hero. Do you remember when we saw the Mike Tyson fight at (cool breeze) house "Mr. Holton?" Uncle Buddy, you and Aunt Dale taught me silence is louder than words, and the meaning of class. You were wearing boots with heels in the early 80s wow!!!! Uncle Anthony, you and Aunt Angela saw me when everyone else focused on my faults, you pointed out my needs… showed me what family is. Thank you. Uncle Charles, you and me used to watch Kung Fu Cinema Saturday at great-granny's house. Remember when I was in judo class you were encouraging me, knowing that I wasn't half as good as I thought I was… lol!!! Uncle Michael, you are misunderstood so much but your heart is unmatched. I love you Unc!!! Aunt Paulette, you and Uncle Timothy demand laughter and smiles. You have this spirit that I've only seen in Aunt Ella, Aunt Linda, Aunt Dale and Aunt Patricia, it's so welcoming it's miraculous. Aunt Delbra, you remember we used to watch all those scary movies when I was younger. I miss that. Thank you for your support at the hospital. Aunt Janice, you are forgiveness in human form. I regret any pain I've ever caused you and I live through that regret every day. Aunt Patricia, you've been gone too long!!! Every time you come into town I'm never able to catch you. I miss you and I love you so much, you are such an irreplaceable soul…..I saw you finally..lol.

To my brother, like Jacob and Esau we fought since birth. I'm so glad that we are getting it together but we're both a work in progress. William, what can I say, you've been my dude for a long time, let's get this money. Jerry, you are my balance, you are the voice that pushed me to go ahead and release one story out of my vault. David, I am so proud and inspired by you. You are the other half that helped me crack the safe and take a step out on faith to allow the world to see a few of my thoughts… just a few. Mark, young heat rock!! That fire!!! I love you boy!!! You and Jerry are so talented musically and in so many other areas, whatever you put your mind to is counted done in my book. To the rest of the Albrittons, Williams, Owens, Spellmans, Smiths, Sills, Vaughans, I love you all the same, we family!!!

Jay, Tonya, Nicole, and Sadie. Time can not be rewound nor fast forwarded. Regardless of how you see the man I was, became, am now…. I accept my faults. They are many.

Thank you for putting up with me, exercising forgiveness, and most importantly, for the priceless gifts you gave.

Jazmine, you have finally gotten it. The mother you have become required several hard lessons but.... you get it, honest. Morris, you are a fine young man. The world has so many mysteries, challenges, believe in yourself.... honesty is the key. Dasani, you are beautiful inside and out. You are the mirror I look forward to looking in every morning and making better. Waiting on your clothing line. Maria, you are the challenge the world needs to grow and become better. Keep asking those questions. Aniyah Brianne Symphony... God's favored. There are so many stories in your name alone. Continue to listen and grow. You are a miracle.

What up Atlantis, Friendship, 15th and 16th Street, Old Road, Regency, Twin Canal, Greenlakes, Green run, Northridge, Bayside Arms, Lake Edwards, Carrie Park, Young's Park, Norview, The Hole, Park Place, Bad Newz, P-town!!!

HEBREWS CH 13: V 3

Remember the prisoners as if chained with them—those who are mistreated—since you yourselves are in the body also.

2 CORINTHIANS CH12: V.7-9

"My grace is sufficient for thee: for my strength is made perfect in weakness."

Special acknowledgement to my incarcerated brothers:You are not forgotten.You are needed and missed in the home,in our daughters and sons lives,at the voting ballots. You are priceless brilliant minds that are useful,and can evoke change.Jeffery Wilson (Renegade)...so inspirational. Can't wait to see you spread your wings out here.Leonard Whitfield (Ali)... everything good awaits you.

R.I.P.

ROBERT LEE ALBRITTON...the greatest man I've ever known....
miss you so much I avoid anything that would trigger this fact.

ANNIE BELL ALBRITTON

ANNIE MAE ALBRITTON, I miss your prayers, kisses and sweet rolls.

JUSTINE SADIE FISCARO,I am numb…..I pray you have found peace.I will let Aniyah know the beauty we shared.

MORRIS VAUGHAN,..we didn't get enough time….ELAINE VAUGHAN, I miss your brutal honesty… seems lies are the "in" thing but not us!!! EVELYN OVERTON, there is so much I didn't understand. Family doesn't start or stop with DNA. PAT BENJAMIN, I see Bobo all the time. You are gravely missed. AUNT ROSE, AUNT BEBE, AUNT CARRIE, AUNT SALLY, AUNT HERLEE, AUNT MARY, COUSIN CARRIE... I miss you all. Everyone and place on this page played a significant part in my molding. My accomplishments are merely a reflection of this.

Historic Seatack Captions

Grandparents...Seatack pioneers.

Albritton family.

Adult family.

Atlantis Apartments.

Murr lee...an angel on earth.

Friendship Village.

Saint Stephen's Church

First house Robert built.

House built from bricks Robert made.

Seatack park.

Recreation Center

Long overdo.

ABOUT THE AUTHOR

M.E. WAS RAISED IN VIRGINIA Beach, Virginia. He is a proud father who wants to change the world one book at a time, while sharing the heritage and history of the area from an overlooked, unseen, and unheard perspective.

Printed in the United States
By Bookmasters